COPYRIGHT

Copyright © 2022 by Ashley Emma
 All rights reserved.
 Farm photo on cover by Lou Bruno
 No portion of this book may be reproduced in any form without written permission from the publisher or author, except as permitted by U.S. copyright law.

Contents

Title Page	VII
1. Chapter One	1
2. Chapter Two	18
3. Chapter Three	30
4. Chapter Four	36
5. Chapter Five	46
6. Chapter Six	52
7. Chapter Seven	58
8. Chapter Eight	63
9. Chapter Nine	73
10. Chapter Ten	80
11. Chapter Eleven	88
12. Chapter Twelve	92
13. Chapter Thirteen	108
14. Chapter Fourteen	112
15. Chapter Fifteen	122
16. Chapter Sixteen	131
17. Chapter Seventeen	140

18. Chapter Eighteen	148
19. Chapter Nineteen	157
20. Chapter Twenty	161
21. Chapter Twenty-one	172
22. Chapter Twenty-two	179
23. Chapter Twenty-three	184
24. Chapter Twenty-four	193
25. Chapter Twenty-five	204
26. Chapter Twenty-six	210
27. Chapter Twenty-seven	218
About the Author (Ashley Emma)	222
All of Ashley Emma's Books on Amazon	227
Excerpt of Abraham and Sarah's Amish Baby	239

Novels by Ashley Emma on Amazon
USA Today Bestselling Author

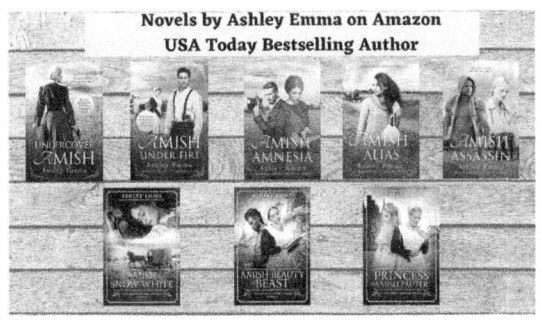

GET 4 OF ASHLEY EMMA'S AMISH EBOOKS FOR FREE

www.AshleyEmmaAuthor.com

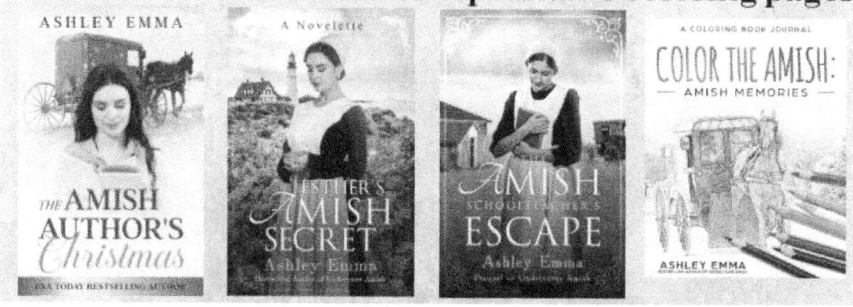

The Amish Prodigal Son

Book 5 of the Amish Bible Story Series

Ashley Emma

Chapter One

Eighteen-year-old Evelyn Yoder smoothed her navy-blue dress and took one last look at the small mirror on her dresser. Her white prayer *kapp* was tied neatly on her head; no hair was out of place. But, of course, she loved to let out a tendril or two in the presence of Theo Glick so he could admire it.

One day while they'd been walking near the pond, she'd enjoyed the way his eyes had trailed from the top of her head to the end of her knee-length blonde hair when she'd let her hair down in his presence, even though she knew it was not allowed. And when he had run his fingers through her hair, she'd been transported.

Evelyn was an Amish girl from Unity, Maine. She loved her community and should abide by the rules, including covering her head properly—even if it meant not seeing that wistful look on Theo's face more often that made her heart pound. But sometimes, she couldn't resist. Now she was eighteen, an adult, and she knew she should not give into that temptation again. It was scandalous behavior.

"Evelyn, hurry up, or I'm coming to your room to drag you out of the house," Livia, her best friend, called from the living room downstairs. The humor in her voice was obvious.

Evelyn wondered what new tactics her friend would invent this time around to get her to stop reading and get her out of the house. She was already immune to every other thing Livia had tried. Still, she lingered. She usually came up to the room whenever Livia visited, and they had to leave the house together. Then her friend would use different methods to make Evelyn leave within ten minutes. It was a game they played frequently. She glanced at the wall clock. All she had to do was wait for ten more minutes.

She looked around her room once more. Her closet was spick and span. Her lavender, navy, gray, black, and brown dresses hung from hangers. The bed was made perfectly. Sunlight streamed in from the window, landing on the multicolored quilt, which had been a gift from Livia to lighten up her room with brighter shades.

She grabbed a hardcover from the books neatly stacked on the table beside her bed; she would read it in little snippets of time when she waited for Theo and Steven or was riding in a buggy with her mother to the local supermarket. There were only four unread ones left from the dozen used books she'd bought at the local bookstore a few weeks ago. She made a mental note to go to the bookstore to purchase new hardcovers or paperbacks before she finished reading her stack of unread books.

The door creaked and swung open. Livia peeped in, her prayer *kapp* slightly askew on her head. Livia was the opposite of Evelyn. She had a flexible, loud, and lively personality that contrasted with her friend's quiet and firm demeanor. In addition, Livia's petite five-feet-two-inch frame made Evelyn six inches taller than her, and Livia's dark hair and eyes were the opposite of Evelyn's golden strands and calm, blue-gray eyes.

Livia's forehead creased into a frown. Her eyes grew round in amazement. "Why are you reading, Eve? Let's go. Steven and Theo are waiting for us."

Quickly looking at the clock before Livia would notice, Evelyn placed the book on her lap and clasped her hands in front of it, grinning.

"Oh, you won't win this one," Livia suddenly said, tickling her under her armpit. "I will get you to put that book away and leave this house."

Evelyn couldn't help it. She burst into laughter, trying to release herself from Livia's grasp.

"Please," she begged, "stop tickling me, and we'll leave the house."

"No. Promise that you'll come out of this room this second, go straight downstairs, grab the basket of pastries, and leave the house. Then, you'll ride down the street to give Mr. and Mrs. Glick and their two boys what you prepared for them."

"I promise. I'll do all you've said, and I won't delay for one second," Evelyn said, laughing.

Livia nodded in satisfaction and let her go. She intertwined her arm in Evelyn's, and they walked out of the room smiling. Evelyn's *daed* and her two older brothers—Elijah and Joe—had left early in the morning to work at their friend Dominic's construction company where they were employed. Her *maem* had gone for a church women's group meeting. Their absence had given her an hour to read without interruption.

Evelyn and Livia went into the kitchen and filled their basket with cinnamon buns, apple dumplings, pies, donuts, and other goodies, covering them with a cloth. The basket was for the Glicks, and the boxes of baked goods they filled were ordered by Amish families and local markets.

In truth, Theo was Evelyn's motivation for baking the treats, but she wasn't too eager to make her intentions known without being sure of his feelings towards her. Theo and Evelyn were childhood friends and had spent time together in each other's houses. Their families were closely knit, making them act like brother and sister despite not being related. It wasn't until she turned seventeen that she noticed her growing attraction to Theo and the way she'd started gravitating towards him. Now at eighteen years old, she hoped he felt the same way and didn't see her as only a friend.

Standing in front of the living room's wooden stove to keep herself warm, she put on her mittens, long stockings, and snow boots. She shrugged into a long woolen coat, and they walked out of the house to carry the goods to the buggy, which took a few trips.

A light dusting of snow lined the lane and covered the fields, giving a white overcast to the trees. A gray and white bird chirped loudly from a treetop. After they finished loading the buggy, Evelyn took the family's horse from the barn. After hitching the horse to the buggy and stroking his mane lovingly, she sat in front and took the reins. The buggy was enclosed with doors and a windshield, but the winter cold still seeped in.

She was grateful she'd hounded her older siblings to teach her to drive until they'd agreed in a bid to stop her persistent nagging. Now she drove the buggy down the street, passing lines of white, maroon, and neutral-colored houses.

Still thinking about her feelings for Theo, she said, "Livia, how can I tell if someone cares for me as much as I care for him?"

Her friend gave her a quizzical look, then smiled. "Evelyn is finally admitting that she's in love with Theo Glick."

Evelyn straightened, keeping very still so as not to betray any emotions on her face. Was she that obvious? From the corner of her eye, she saw Livia's lips curve into a grin.

"I knew it. It's about time. So, are you planning on telling him?" Livia asked.

"What? How did you know? I've always denied it when you asked me." Evelyn could feel her cheeks heating up as Livia's statement brought Theo's image to the front of her mind. He had brown curly hair, gray eyes, high cheekbones, and a chiseled jaw, and he was a few inches taller than her. Theo had the right mixture of confidence and playfulness that drew her to him no matter how much she resisted.

"Yes, you've always denied it, but I know you've been in love with him since we were teens. Please, answer the question," Livia demanded. "When are you going to tell him?"

"Oh, I don't think I can. We've been friends for so long, and what if I ruin that and make things awkward? How do I know if he loves me back?" Evelyn asked.

"Well, you can tell from his actions. That's what my *maem* always says."

Evelyn cast her thoughts back to all the times she'd seen Theo recently. His actions towards her weren't different. He still talked to her in the same manner and didn't treat her any differently. Did he still see her as a good friend, maybe even a sister, or was he just hiding how he felt? Could he possibly love her like she loved him?

She swallowed. She wasn't sure she was willing to let go of her feelings for Theo if he didn't feel the same way. "What if he doesn't love me?"

"You won't know until you tell him how you feel, but he'd be crazy not to love you. Just tell him. What's the worst that can happen?"

Evelyn veered into an uneven lane that led to Theo's family's farm.

"I hope he sees me the same way I see him. I see myself married to him and living in love and happiness," she said, staring at the horizon where it seemed the blue sky met the dark green trees. "But if I'm wrong and he only sees me as a friend, it will be awkward between us."

"Evelyn, isn't it worth the risk? Wouldn't you rather ask and face possible rejection rather than keep wondering?"

She turned to Livia, then looked away. She wasn't yet ready to make public her feelings for Theo. Today, she'd try to find out what he felt towards her. "You're right, Livia. It is worth the risk."

"What about Steven? Have you ever had feelings for Steven?" Livia asked.

She huffed. Although Steven was Theo's younger brother, he was definitely not Theo. "No. I could never feel like that about him. He's like a brother to me."

Livia shook her head and chuckled. "Of course not. You've been pining for Theo. If he has an ounce of sense, he'll like you back."

The Glicks' farm was massive. Ivan Glick had dozens of acres of land with sheep, cows, and horses. Snow draped across the peak of the barn, sparkling in the sunlight.

Evelyn's buggy rumbled down the driveway, then she parked in front of the farmhouse, where Theo's father shoveled snow off the land. Spotting Theo and Steven working in the yard, she grabbed the Glick's basket and came down from the buggy with Livia right behind her.

"Good morning, Mr. Glick, Theo, and Steven," she said cheerfully as she walked into the house to greet Linda Glick, Theo's mother, and give her the baked goods.

"Good morning, ladies," Mr. Glick called. Theo and Steven waved to her before Evelyn and Livia waved back, then went inside and shut the door.

Mrs. Glick let them inside. "It's good to see you," she said, smoothing wisps of her gray hair back into her prayer *kapp*. She ran her hands down the front of her apron-covered lavender dress, and her gray eyes crinkled into a smile. "What did you bring today?"

"Some of the boys' favorites," Evelyn said, giving her the basket.

"Oh, you know how my sons love your cinnamon rolls," Linda said with a grin. "And Ivan loves your pie. You're going to make your husband a very happy man one day, Evelyn."

"She sure will," Livia added, giving her friend a knowing grin, which only deepened the blush that had spread out on Evelyn's cheeks.

"Thank you, Mrs. Glick," Evelyn replied softly.

"This is for you, dear." Linda handed Evelyn raw, organic milk and meat straight from the farm. On occasion, Evelyn would give Linda as much baked goods as she could while the older woman would return the gesture with her farm milk, meat, or produce for the Yoders. Sometimes, Linda brought goods for Evelyn's mother without asking for anything in return. At other times, it was Evelyn's family who extended the hand of generosity.

Thanking Linda, Evelyn took the items and put them in the buggy, then she walked up to Theo and Steven. Livia was already laughing at something Steven was saying. As soon as Evelyn approached, the two brothers straightened and turned their attention to her.

Theo and Steven looked so alike and were so close in age that they could pass for twins. Steven's shorter height, an oval face, and green eyes were the only physical differences between them, and Theo was more broad-shouldered.

Behaviorally, they were opposites. Even now, Theo's face was filled with lightness. His lips twitched as if holding back a smile just for Evelyn. He had an aura that made her want to hug him, whereas Steven was solemn and focused. His eyes pierced Evelyn in a way that made her slightly uncomfortable as he strode toward her. Theo gestured for her to come over at the same time.

"Good morning," she said to both of them. Her eyes were on Theo, her feet moving towards him.

"Good morning," they chorused.

"I've been meaning to talk to you," Steven said, intercepting her before Theo could take over her attention with conversation.

She blinked and focused on him. "About what?"

Steven looked around at his brother and Livia, who were watching them. "It's not something I can say here. Can we..."

"Can we talk about it later?" she interrupted. She wanted to give Steven an audience, but at the moment, she needed to sort out her feelings towards Theo and know his stance.

"*Ja.* How about getting hot chocolate at four at the coffee shop?"

She shrugged, wondering what was so important that Steven wanted to say it today. "Of course. I'll meet you there."

He inclined his head in a slight nod before turning to help his father. "I'm going to help my father with the shoveling."

"I'm going inside to help Mrs. Glick," Livia said, giving Evelyn another knowing look before going to the house.

Goosebumps covered Evelyn's arms as she walked over to Theo. The moment her eyes connected with his, everything she'd planned to tell him flew away from her mind.

"Hi," she said, unable to form any other coherent sentence.

He cocked his head to the side, regarding her. His eyes peered at her thoughtfully in that way that made her heart lurch and beat ten times faster. "Do you mind us going inside the barn? I'd like us to talk in private."

She looked at the barn, then at Ivan, wondering what Theo's father would think if she went off with his son to talk in an enclosed space.

"Let's go to the side of the barn instead," she said, knowing that nobody would see them there. Still, it was less scandalous than talking indoors alone when they weren't married.

"Evelyn, I'd like you to accompany me on Rumspringa," he said, getting straight to the point when they reached the side of the barn.

She paused, stunned. Why would he ask her such a thing? Although Rumspringa was a period set out for young people to explore the outside world and decide whether they wanted to join the Amish church or not, some youths took the opportunity to engage in drinking, partying, or even drugs. Sometimes these young folks ended up coming home and repenting when they realized the error of their ways, yet they could have avoided asking for God's forgiveness if they had abided by the rules in the first place.

Evelyn didn't believe Theo would do those types of things, but a whiff of suspicion settled in her mind. Theo might want her as a girlfriend only during Rumspringa, or he just wanted to have fun with her. She would never participate in such immoral activities.

"Are you asking me to go with you?" she demanded. "You know I have no intention of going on Rumspringa. I know I want to join the Amish church, so I don't see a need for it."

She didn't like the idea of Rumspringa. She wasn't interested in many activities outside of reading, singing, church activities, and house chores, and she preferred to avoid rambunctious crowds.

"No, it's much more than that. Ever since you gave me that dashing smile on your seventeenth birthday, I've fallen..." he stammered, and her heart lurched as she wondered if he really did have feelings for her after all. Could it be true? He continued, "I want to be with you, Evelyn, to see your dimples when you smile. I want you to be by my side throughout our lifetime."

Theo held her hand in his, sending tingles up her spine. He liked her dimples? Not only that, he wanted to spend his life with her? She froze, barely believing he was saying such things to her, things she'd hoped he would say to her for so long. It was finally happening, and she was so stunned, she couldn't even speak. Instead, she listened intently.

"I've got other dreams to fulfill as well during Rumspringa, but I'm asking you to join me. Come explore the world with me, Evelyn." He squeezed her hand.

Her breath hitched in her chest as she focused on breathing in and out. Her heart pounded in her ears, and it took her so long to get a word out that a concerned look shadowed his face.

"Are you alright, Evelyn?" he asked.

"Oh, yes, I'm fine. This is a shock, that's all. What dream do you want to fulfill?" she asked, finally managing to speak.

He looked away. "It's complicated."

"If you don't tell me, how do you expect me to accept what I don't know?"

"I'm not asking you to accept anything now, Eve. I'm asking you to think about it. Imagine going on Rumspringa with me and then moving things forward from there. Who knows, I might let go of those dreams. Then it will be an ordinary Rumspringa with just the two of us. We can travel, go to the movies, and do innocent *Englisher* activities. Nothing immoral. Afterward, if you'll have me, we'll court and live happily ever after."

Evelyn closed her eyes, imagining a happily ever after with Theo. They'd have lots of children, and she'd be a homemaker.

Evelyn was in love with him, and he'd shown her that he had similar feelings by asking her to accompany him, but she'd never intended to go on Rumspringa. Maybe he wanted to see the extent of her attraction, or he aimed to strengthen their bond before officially courting and marrying her.

"Why don't we just skip Rumspringa altogether and stay here?" she asked.

"Don't you want to experience life outside of the community?" he asked passionately. "Don't you want to see what it's like to drive a car, own a cell phone without keeping it a secret, or wear *Englisher* clothing?"

"Do you have a secret cell phone, Theo Glick?" Evelyn asked, hands on her hips.

He gave a mischievous smile. "Many of the young folks do, you know. I'm not the only one."

She smiled, shaking her head, then sighed. "I need to think about this, Theo. I can't give you an answer right now."

"That's all I ask. Just think about it," Theo said.

She went into the house to get Livia, then they climbed into the buggy.

"What happened?" Livia asked curiously.

"I'll tell you on the way," Evelyn said as they rode away from the farm.

"Girlfriend? You want me to be your girlfriend?" Evelyn asked, stunned, staring at the young man sitting across from her who looked so much like Theo but who was also so different from his brother. Their mugs of hot chocolate were half-gone and now forgotten about.

"Yes, will you be my girlfriend?" Steven gave her a shy smile.

Evelyn shivered despite the warm temperature of the place. She gave Steven a once over discreetly. Two brothers had indicated an interest in her, but she could only choose one. While Steven was reliable, hardworking, loyal, and the person who would most likely stand by someone in times of crisis, he was blunt and went straight to the point. On the other hand, Theo was a people person and a smooth talker but was reckless and impulsive. Did he even plan to be baptized into the Amish church?

What if he left for Rumspringa and never came back? Evelyn gulped, her throat going dry at the mere thought of it. Perhaps she should go with him, after all, to keep him in check.

"Evelyn?" Steven asked, peering at her and bringing her back to the here and now.

"I'm sorry. I'm just shocked. Why do you want me to be your girlfriend?" she said, hoping to find a loophole in his reply that would enable her to reject his offer.

His eyes lit up. "Do you remember your fifteenth birthday? Who wished you happy birthday first, Theo or me?"

She tried to recollect and realized that Steven had made the extra effort to make her birthday special the past few years. "You did. You wished me a happy birthday and sang a song to me."

He smiled. "How about when you turned sixteen and seventeen?"

"You gave me gifts."

He brought out his hand and placed it on hers. A warm feeling grew in Evelyn, confusing her. Suddenly realizing his bold move, he withdrew his hand. What if someone saw them? The warmth seeped out of Evelyn.

Steven seemed unfazed. "You're beautiful, Eve. You have a good heart, too. You take care of those around you in a calm, unassuming manner. I've always admired you and feel my heart tug whenever you're around. Since we'll both be turning eighteen soon, I'd like us to be boyfriend and girlfriend, if you want."

What did she want? What if her feelings were just that—only feelings that were fleeting?

Evelyn knew the answer to Steven's request, but one look at his hopeful expression made her not want to dash his hopes by saying no immediately. The feelings Theo and Steven's touch gave her were different. While Theo's touch made her alive and filled her with romantic longing, holding Steven's hand gave her the warm, comfortable feeling of friendship.

For a brief moment, she wondered if she was wrong. She wasn't experienced in affairs of the heart and didn't know much about them. She'd always thought that Steven was like a brother to her, nothing more. But now he'd told her about his romantic feelings, and she wondered if she also felt different. What did she know about love, after all? What if she was wrong about the way she felt?

Although she wanted to choose Theo, he was impulsive and flighty. On the other hand, Steven had shown her steady care over the years. She wondered if that meant he would be a better husband in the long run.

The fact that the two brothers had talked to her about their feelings on the same day made matters even more confusing. She resolved to pray about the matter before making a decision. If she sought advice, she'd know what her true feelings were or at least find a nice way to let one of them down.

"Can I think about it? I don't want to rush into making a decision," she said.

"Of course. You should think about what I've said before making a decision. I'll feel better if I knew that you also prayed about it before saying yes or no to me."

"Of course." She plastered a smile on her face and averted her eyes. She bent to adjust her *kapp* so he wouldn't notice that her expression was fake. They drank their now room-temperature cocoa in silence afterward.

When they were finished, Steven dropped her off at Livia's house. Evelyn said a hasty goodbye, hurried to the house and greeted her friend's large family.

Livia had five sisters and four brothers. Her family was comprised of twelve people—her parents and ten children. The walls of their house were painted various colors such as blue and yellow, making the house seem as warm as summer even in the dead of winter.

Evelyn found Livia in the kitchen with her siblings, playing Rook. Her friend thumped her hand on the table in victory and laughed, making several of her siblings jump and giggle.

"I won again!" she cried triumphantly.

"Livia," Evelyn said, inclining her head to the door to signal that she wanted to talk to her alone.

"You better go, Livia," one of her sisters said. "Your leaving will give one of us the chance to win."

"Not for long," Livia called, then the girls found an empty room and locked the door for privacy.

"What is it, Eve? You look worried," Livia asked, concern in her voice.

"So, you know how Theo asked me to go on Rumspringa this morning at the farm?" she asked, her cheeks heated up. She was sure they'd turned bright red.

Livia grinned. "You're so blessed to have a good man like Theo notice you." She paused. "Wait. What happened? Did he just ask you to be his girlfriend?"

Evelyn shook her head. "No, that was Steven."

Livia stepped back, a bewildered expression on her face. "Steven? I thought we were talking about Theo."

"Steven and I just went on a date where he asked me to be his girlfriend. Theo asked me to be with him at Rumspringa this morning. It all happened on the same day." She went on to tell Livia the details of her talk with Steven.

"Oh," Livia said, then crossed her arms over her chest. "It seems like Steven is much more serious about his feelings for you. Maybe I should go talk to Theo."

Evelyn smiled at her friend's protectiveness. "There's no need to talk to him. You don't have to act like my older sister."

"I am your best friend. Close enough," she said, smiling as they each sat down at the table. She held Evelyn's hands in hers. "What do you want to do? You have two brothers who are both in love with you."

"I'm confused, Livia. I don't think Theo is serious. He just wants me to follow him to Rumspringa, then see how it goes and possibly consider a future together. Theo jumps in first, then thinks later." She heaved a sigh. "On the other hand, Steven knows what he wants and made me realize he's been in love with me for several years. I just didn't see it. He's also reliable, hard-working, and committed. He has traits any woman would like in her husband."

"Who does your heart want, Eve?" Livia asked intensely, peering into her friend's eyes.

"Theo," Evelyn blurted, then grimaced. "I'm not sure he wants me in the same way, though. I thought maybe he did, but I think he's just looking for someone to run around with on Rumspringa."

"Oh, Eve, I see the way he looks at you. I think he wants you, too. Maybe he hasn't realized how much he wants you yet."

"What if he just wants me as his Rumspringa date and nothing more?"

"Theo wouldn't do that. You can find out how serious he is. Just ask him if he wants you to be his girlfriend or if he really wants to wait until later to court you. Or you can say that you'll only be a girlfriend to someone who loves you, not just wanting you to follow him around. His answer will help you know his thoughts about you. You'll be able to gauge his seriousness then and give him an appropriate response."

Evelyn nodded. "You're right. I'm going to do it."

"Who knows what he feels? We can only assume. Please choose carefully, Eve. And choose your words wisely when you answer Theo and Steven. If Theo has feelings for you, gently tell Steven that you two aren't the right fit so he won't be so devastated."

Although Theo had spoken cryptically about his dreams, Evelyn hoped Livia was right. She hoped that Theo had the same feelings as she did. Closing her eyes, Evelyn mumbled a quick prayer to God to help her make the right choice. She prayed for Theo to be that choice—it was her heart's desire.

She thanked her friend and went home where she spent the rest of the day praying about what to do.

Chapter Two

"It is not the Amish way."

Theodore Glick stared at his father, Ivan, through slitted eyelids as they mucked stalls and cleaned the barn. He wished his father had not repeated his favorite mantra. Unfortunately, it wasn't easy to convince Ivan otherwise once he started talking about the Amish way.

"*Daed*," he said, making sure his tone was extremely respectful and calm. "It's just for a few years. Surely the Amish will understand that I want to serve my country."

Since he was a child, Theo had wanted to become a soldier. His desire to join the US Army had begun when Sergeant Ethan Mills, a veteran soldier, had moved into the apartment a few miles away and boasted about his military feats to anyone who cared to listen. Theo had seen himself serving his country honorably and joked about it, only for other members of the Amish community to hush him. As he grew older, his dream crystallized into an unquenchable burning desire he thought of day and night.

Before turning eighteen, he'd tried to convince his father to give him signed permission to join the Army, but Ivan had refused. Theo was an adult now and didn't need the signature. He'd already planned out how he'd become a soldier in a few months. He'd thought that if he kept using convincing words on his father, Ivan would eventually relent and understand why he wanted to serve his country.

Today, he'd been at his best behavior, taking on more farm duties than he'd normally do. He'd been working since morning and even made Steven rest when he'd complained of a headache. But that had not changed Ivan's mind.

He leaned on the rake he'd been using to clear out the barn and watched his father carefully, hoping that he'd used the right words to persuade him.

"Why don't we like our members leaving the community, Theo?" Ivan asked, sitting down on a stool to catch his breath.

Theo smiled. He knew the answer to that one. "So that we can all act in the Amish way," he replied, throwing his father's words back to him.

"And what's the Amish way?"

"To live a quiet and peaceful life, displaying discipleship and good works. That's why I want to join the military. I want to show my good works by serving America."

"The military kills people, Theo. The Lord says not to kill. You are foolish to think that you would be doing good works. How can you be serving God while serving in the military?"

"I'd be protecting my country, *Daed*," Theo argued.

"We're here on earth to serve *God*. Our faith calls for a life filled with good works *within* the church. That life should be separate from the world. I'm sure you remember Romans 12:1-2."

Knowing Ivan's next request from experience, Theo released an exasperated sigh and recited the verses. "Do not be conformed to this world... Yes, I know those verses. You've made me recite them hundreds of times."

The barn door squeaked. Steven walked in, making Theo pause. Steven's eyes went from Ivan to Theo, then he walked to his father.

"*Daed*, I feel better now. You can go in and rest. You and Theo can complete your discussion in the farmhouse."

Ivan rubbed his back and stood up, then continued mucking the stalls. "Thank you. I still need to exercise my bones, or they'll become brittle and unusable."

"*Daed*," Theo said, calling his father's attention to his eagerness to continue the conversation. "I'm sure there is a way to be in the Army and still serve God."

"It's not possible when there is killing and violence involved. Theo, we separate ourselves from the world completely. That is our way. Besides, if you go to the Army, will you truly not conform to this world?"

"I won't. I'll still live the Amish way. I promise." Theo put a hand over his heart.

"I can already predict what you'll do from your present behavior. You hardly ever put in your share of work on the farm except on Mondays, and we both know why that is—it's to impress a certain someone who visits. Today, you have only worked this long because you hope to convince me to accept your leaving the Amish and joining the Army, an organization filled with violence and killing."

Theo's lips twitched in embarrassment at his father's reminder of his working every Monday until he saw Evelyn, and she left. Although he was the more muscular son, inheriting his father's physique, he'd always known that farming didn't suit him. The work was endless and tiring. It wasn't the same as serving in the Army, which would be so much more rewarding.

"Theo," his father said, ruffling his hair. "I'm not asking you to be like Steven or work on the farm from day till night, but you need to learn a thing or two about responsibility. Besides, I don't want you to experience all the violence that comes with active duty in the Army; it will change you. I don't want to lose you. What if something happens to you out there?" He looked at Steven, then at Theo, his eyes filled with affection. "I want my two sons by my side, living this peaceful and quiet life. Remember that Proverbs 22:6 says, 'Train up a child in the way that he should go; and when he is old, he will not depart from it.' I hope I've ingrained Amish principles in you, and I don't want you to cast them aside."

Theo's heart constricted. He'd come here to tell Ivan that he'd be leaving for the Army in a few months, but the look in his father's eyes made him want to remain in this Amish community in Unity, Maine. How could he break his heart now?

"I..." The words congealed in his mouth. He forced himself to talk. Straightening his shoulders and looking his father square in the eye in his best show of confidence, he said, "I want to join the Army, and I intend to do so."

A hard thumping sound from Steven's direction made him turn. His brother had dropped a bucket on the floor, raising clouds of dust and dirt in the air. Ivan barely flinched as he stood still and quiet, eyes closed. He mumbled a prayer Theo couldn't hear.

The sun was setting. Outside the barn, the cows mooed, and the horses neighed as if they knew it was time to take them inside. Theo would have reveled in the comforting sounds if he wasn't having a faceoff with his father.

"Do you remember the story of the prodigal son?" Ivan asked.

Theo cocked his head to the side regarding his father. He read the Holy Book sparingly, only opening the pages when absolutely necessary. He remembered some of the Sunday sermons Bishop Johnson preached and could recite a few Bible verses his *maem* had taught him. Of course, he knew the story. At least, he had heard it before, but did he understand its true meaning?

"It's a parable of Jesus," Theo said, but that was all he could recall. He didn't know the story's true meaning, so he kept silent.

"A man had two sons. One day the younger son came to him and said, 'Father, give me my inheritance so I can live my life.' The man was sad and tried to convince his son not to go. He eventually gave up when the son insisted, handed the boy's inheritance over, and watched him leave. The son traveled to a different country and squandered all the money. When he had nothing left to eat, he went to work on a pig farm."

"I won't do that, *Daed*," Theo said, not wanting to hear the story of the irresponsible son or find out what had befallen him. "I'll serve America faithfully. I'll be given a medal of honor, you'll see. Then, I'll come back and do whatever you want."

Ivan's eyes filled with sadness. His voice became a deep well of pain.

"You might have the capacity to make the country proud, but will you serve God faithfully? If you become a soldier—and I hope you don't—will you be separate from the world, or will you conform to all its evils and temptations? Fulfilling your dream of going to the Army might break you. You will witness so much violence, but killing others with your own hands might make you have the worst nightmares."

He leaned toward Theo, standing shoulder to shoulder, and whispered, "I know you. I understand you, son. You put up a carefree front, making everyone feel that you're confident." Ivan turned and touched Theo's chest. "But deep down, you're soft. You crave love and acceptance. You want to be relevant, but you can be relevant to God in the Amish way."

Theo bunched his hands into fists. He let his nails dig into his palms, fighting the truth of his father's words. Ivan was right, yet Theo needed to experience things for himself. He didn't want to live a life full of regret and ask himself what could have been. He shook off the suggestive whispers in his mind asking him to give in to his father's will.

"This is my dream. It's what I've always wanted to do, and there's nothing you can do to change it," Theo stated proudly.

There was silence for a few seconds. "You shouldn't talk to me in that way," Ivan said quietly.

"I'm sorry," Theo replied flatly. He could feel the determination coursing through him. He knew that his father would see the fire in his eyes. "But I must do this."

"Have you counted the cost of your leaving? Your family is here. We need you."

"You'll all be fine without me," he said, voice rising. "You even admitted yourself I'm not much help on the farm."

With the situation escalating, Theo wasn't sure he'd ever get Ivan's approval to join the Army. He wanted his father to show some sign of understanding even if he didn't outrightly approve of his leaving. Still, nothing had come of his staying all these months and applying various persuasive methods. Well, he was eighteen—an adult in the eyes of America and the world. He could do whatever he liked.

"Everyone will be fine without me," he said with a stubborn set of his shoulders.

Ivan shook his head, his face etched in disappointment. "I hope you change your mind. You belong here in Unity." Then he left the barn and shut the door.

Theo forcibly booted a pile of dirt at the corner into a stall, scattering dust and hay around his feet. Steven cleared his throat loudly from behind him. Even his younger brother was judging him. He turned to his brother, but Steven had already opened his mouth to speak.

"*Daed* is right. You should stay. Please, don't go. We need you here. You'll break their hearts if you go."

Theo angrily marched out of the barn and walked to the farmhouse. It was one thing to listen to the commanding tone of his father; it was an entirely different thing to hear similar words from his younger brother.

By the time he held the doorknob, Theo had realized that if he got into the house, he'd have to walk through the living room where his father and mother were probably talking about him. He wasn't sure he could ignore the sadness he'd see in his mother's eyes. So, he turned away and flounced his way off the farm with a brisk walk. Steven could herd the animals into the barn.

Thoughts of anger and determination intertwined in his mind as he walked down the street with no specific destination. He'd have left months ago if he hadn't feared breaking his parents' hearts. He wanted to visit them frequently while serving in the Army, but he knew if he left, they might break all contact with him and shun him even though he hadn't been baptized into the church yet.

He kept walking until he realized he was standing in front of Evelyn's house. The sky had darkened. The stars and moon were bright, casting shadows on the house. He walked around to the back of the house and stopped close to Evelyn's window.

They wouldn't miss him much, he hoped. Steven put in the bulk of the work at the farm. Theo's input was little compared to his brother's except when Evelyn was visiting the farm. When she was there, he worked hard to impress her.

Theo looked up at Evelyn's window and its drawn curtains. She could be sleeping, or maybe she wasn't in her room. She'd miss him if he left without her. Theo wanted Evelyn to come with him. They could get married in an *Englisher* church and be together for the rest of their lives.

Images of what had occurred that evening played in his mind. Remembering the story of the prodigal son, a thought occurred to him. A plan formed in his mind, and he smiled. First, he'd ask Sergeant Ethan Mills to help him. The veteran soldier enthusiastically repeated his war stories every time he met Theo. Once the sergeant agreed to help him out, Theo's plan to join the military would be set in motion.

He turned and started the long walk home.

Within the next few days, Theo spoke to Sergeant Ethan Mills and discovered that the preparation to join the military would be intense. Since the Amish stopped schooling at eighth grade, he didn't have a high school diploma, so he would have to get a GED certificate—the equivalent of a high school diploma. He would also need to take a vocational aptitude battery test (ASVAB) and meet physical requirements before starting basic training in the Army.

Sergeant Ethan Mills was eager to help him in any way possible. Theo secretly went to the Englisher's house to read and go through numerous exercise routines.

At home, he studied for the GED by the light of his battery-operated lantern at night or locked his room door when he had to study during the day so that his plan would remain a secret. He didn't like schoolwork, but it was a small price he was willing to pay.

Winter ended. The snow on the sidewalks thawed. Spring was underway with frequent rain and growing grass for the animals to graze before Theo made another request. On that day, his mother had gone to the farmer's market. His father was alone in the living room, and Theo made some tea. The aroma was relaxing, leaving a sweet tang on his tongue. He hoped it would do the same to his father. When he took the tea to the living room, Ivan smiled.

"Theo, what do you want? You don't need to do all these nice things for me."

Theo's eyes flicked away in embarrassment. "I know. It's just that I don't think you'll like the idea, *Daed*."

"Go ahead, say it. I'll listen to you."

He cleared his throat and sat down, hoping his father would buy the lie he was about to tell. "I know you're opposed to me leaving the Amish, and I understand your concerns. I'm sorry for troubling you about it earlier. I've thought about it and realize that you're right. We should be separate from the world, serving God in all honesty and truth."

Ivan scrutinized him for a few seconds, then smiled.

"Of course, my son. You're still young and have the itch to see the world, so it might be hard to agree with all the Amish rules." A look of suspicion crossed his face. "What made you change your mind so suddenly?"

Theo had been expecting that. He straightened in his chair and started weaving a more intricate web of lies.

"The real reason why I wanted to go into the Army is that it would have made me independent and command respect from other people." At least, that part was true. He tried to look as relaxed as possible as he continued: "If I can build my own house and have a farm at a young age, I'll be admired in the Amish community and still be independent."

Ivan nodded. Theo leaned closer.

"You can help by splitting the farm between Steven and me so I can fulfill my new dream. We could divide it in two."

Ivan drew back, suspicion clouding his features. "You want me to split the farm into two?"

"You don't need to do that. Just give me the monetary share of my farm inheritance. I'll buy land somewhere else, in the Amish community, of course. Then I'll farm, build my house, and start a family."

"The prodigal son story," Ivan said in a quiet tone. "Is that where you got this idea from?"

Theo closed his eyes, hoping that Ivan would agree to his request. "Yes, *Daed*. I know it's not a good example to follow, but it's a win-win for both of us. You get your wish since I'll remain Amish, and I get my independence and honor."

"Why would I give you an inheritance while I'm still alive?"

"Fathers help their sons build houses, get jobs, and raise their families. Isn't that giving their sons some sort of inheritance?" he said in a desperate rush.

He hoped his father would give in to his demands before discovering it was a ruse. His mother would be back soon; she could quickly decipher when Theo was lying. If Ivan accepted his request now, Linda wouldn't meet them talking or stop Theo's plans from coming to fruition.

A heavy silence descended on the room and lasted for several minutes. Theo fidgeted in anticipation. Did the plan work? Would his father say yes or refuse again? Ivan stared at the ceiling, saying nothing. Theo finally gave up on getting an affirmative answer and started walking out of the living room.

"I'll consider what you said. Maybe we can find a way, if it will keep you from leaving us," Ivan said.

Theo bowed slightly. "Thank you, *Daed*."

A feeling of freedom and satisfaction settled in him. He tried his best not to smile widely or shout with joy. He'd soon be leaving for the military to fulfill his dreams, and the money for the inheritance would help him if he ever fell into financial troubles. Life couldn't have gotten any better.

A small bit of guilt niggled at the back of his mind, but he ignored it, telling himself it was necessary for him to lie to his family in order to fulfill his dream.

Only one thing weighed on his mind—Evelyn. If he could convince Eve as easily as he'd swayed his father... If she'd only consider leaving the Amish with him, everything would be perfect.

Chapter Three

Ever since Theo's Rumspringa question to Evelyn that he had asked her months ago, she had been trying her best to see him, but he was always in a rush or not at home when she visited the farm. He'd also stopped coming to the Singings the young Amish folks held, which he had used to enjoy.

It made her wonder if Theo was deliberately avoiding her or if he had something urgent to take care of. She had to speak with him soon.

When she'd lost all her patience, she went to Theo's mother. Mrs. Linda Glick was a quiet woman with a gentle demeanor. She was preparing a meal on the woodstove when Evelyn arrived.

"Good afternoon, Mrs. Glick," Evelyn said, sniffing the air and smelling beef stew, probably made with meat and produce from their farm.

"Good afternoon, Evelyn. Are you looking for Theo and Steven? They've gone out."

"I was hoping to see Theo. When will he be back?"

"I don't know. Do you want to leave a message for him?"

"No, I'd rather wait," she said, picking up a knife to help Linda with cutting up the ingredients for a side salad. "I haven't seen Theo around lately. I hope everything is okay."

Linda paused in contemplation, a puzzled look on her face. "Theo is doing fine. He's been out a lot lately, but I thought maybe the two of you were spending time together at your house."

"No, we haven't." She wondered where Theo had been going if his mother thought he'd been visiting her but chose not to dwell on the thought.

At that moment, Theo sauntered into the kitchen, smiling. Sweat beaded on his forehead and trickled down his face. He wiped it off with a handkerchief, he nodded to Evelyn in greeting, and flopped down on a kitchen chair.

Evelyn wondered what Theo had been up to. Maybe Theo had secretly started working somewhere else, like Dominic's construction company. Theo had never seemed eager to work on the farm for his entire life. Was he keeping his new career choice a secret from his parents?

By the time they'd finished preparing the meal, Steven and Ivan were back.

"Evelyn, will you join us for dinner?" Linda asked. "You did help make it, after all."

"I would love to. Thank you," Evelyn said.

They all sat down, bowed their heads, prayed silently, and began to eat. Afterward, Evelyn and Theo went to the porch.

"Eve," Theo said, then fell silent.

"Theo, where have you been? I've been looking for you for days. I didn't see you at home, in the barn, or anywhere else I checked," Evelyn demanded.

He quickly smiled. "I was out. I've been busy with a few things."

"I've thought about what we discussed," she rushed to say before she lost the courage to say what she'd meant to tell him. "And I..."

"Let me drive you home," he interrupted. "We can talk about it in the buggy."

Evelyn blinked and stared at him. Rather than his usual confident, carefree manner, he looked agitated. She wondered if he'd been working too much. "You seem different, Theo. Is anything bothering you? Is this about where you've been going secretly?"

"Yes," he replied shortly and walked to the barn to get a horse.

His behavior made her feel worried. She waited until the buggy began rumbling down the dirt lane before she spoke. "Theo, you can tell me what you've been up to. I can keep a secret."

He stared at her for a while, then shook his head. "Eve, I want to tell you, but some things are better left unsaid. I'll tell you later when the time is right. I have a question, though. How do you see the Amish community?"

"I love it here. It's my home. I enjoy being with my family and going to church, and I'm happy I was born Amish. I can't imagine what I'd have been like if I was born as an *Englisher*," she said, smiling.

He nodded. "So, have you ever thought about leaving the Amish community?"

She jerked away from him, shocked. "What?"

"Not permanently," he said. "I mean on Rumspringa, like we talked about."

"Oh, that again." She wrapped her arms around her waist and scooted as far away from him as possible in the buggy that now felt tiny. "I still don't see why any Amish person would want to leave the community. There's so much evil going on in the world that we're not a part of. We live a peaceful and quiet life."

His shoulders deflated. "You're right. We live a peaceful and quiet life—sometimes too quiet."

"Theo," she said in alarm, "don't say that. Why are you suddenly speaking this way? You didn't get into any trouble, did you?"

"No, I didn't," he said, shrugging.

The look on his face seemed to counter his statement. He turned slightly away from Evelyn and continued driving the buggy, his demeanor becoming standoffish. His hand reached out to touch her *kapp*, then stopped halfway.

"I wish things were different, Eve. Then we could be together," he whispered, eyes focused on the road. "But I can't be with you. It would be selfish of me."

That's when it dawned on Evelyn why Theo had been acting strangely since he'd asked her to accompany him on Rumspringa. He had to reject her because he'd found out that his brother wanted to be with her and decided to cancel his Rumspringa with her out of the selflessness of his heart.

That was such an honorable action. Theo looked out for Steven's feelings and considered those around him above himself. That made him even more endearing and worthy in her eyes. Theo was the kind of man she wanted to marry. He was a selfless man who'd let go of his love interest for his brother.

A painful pang hit her heart because she realized that she desired them to share their life as husband and wife more than ever. But she might not have her wish if Theo was set on the path of giving up their potential courtship to Steven. Could she convince him to change his mind? If she assured him that she loved him and not his brother, maybe he'd consider it.

"Theo, are you saying this because Steven asked me to be his girlfriend? I didn't give him an answer, you know."

"What? No," Theo spat out. "I had no idea he asked you. He never told me." He made a low growling sound in his throat.

"Oh, I see," Evelyn said. "Well, then, why are you saying we can't be together?"

"It's complicated, Evelyn. I can't tell you. I'm so sorry," he said solemnly, a glimmer of anger still shining in his eyes.

"Theo, tell me. Let me try to change your mind."

"There is nothing you can do or say to change my mind," Theo insisted. "My mind has been made up."

"Theo, what is going on? Please, just tell me. I want to be with *you*, Theo," she cried, tears stinging her eyes as she blurted out the desires of her heart. "Please, don't do this."

"I have to go, Evelyn. I'm sorry. You should go inside the house now."

"But Theo—"

"Go inside, Evelyn," Theo snapped, causing her to jump. "Don't try to argue with me about this. I already said my mind has been made up."

Hurt and stunned, Evelyn scrambled out of the buggy before running into her house, hurrying to her room, and throwing herself onto her bed as tears coursed down her cheeks. Why did he say they couldn't be together? Had she done something wrong? She hadn't given Steven an answer yet.

She would have to find a viable reason to make Theo change his mind. Instead, she'd come up with a plan to let Steven down gently and bring Theo closer.

She'd make the two brothers realize that there was only one person her heart pined for.

Chapter Four

Theo rode back to the house feeling more dejected than ever. He let the horse trudge to the farm as he stared ahead, deep in thought. When had Steven asked Evelyn to be his girlfriend, and why hadn't Steven at least let Theo know that he was going to ask her? Evelyn had said she hadn't given Steven an answer—she hadn't told Steven no. Why hadn't she turned him down right away?

Perhaps Evelyn was considering Steven's request. Anger and jealousy burned in Theo's chest at the thought, but he decided not to tell Steven that he knew about it. Maybe they belonged together.

His decision to finally join the military had cost him Eve. He'd had the chance for Evelyn to be his, and he'd withdrawn, sent her off without giving her a chance to speak.

It was obvious that Evelyn had no plans of leaving the Amish. To her, it was sacrilegious to even think about it. She'd moved away from him as if he were a plague when he'd asked her about it again. Her face had been so joyful when she spoke about the benefits of being Amish. It seemed like the community she'd been born into was where she was meant to be. He couldn't bring himself to convince her to leave. It wouldn't be right.

Besides, she was the only daughter of her parents. Her brothers were about to get married, leaving her alone with her mother and father. If he asked her to leave the Amish against her will, what would that say of him?

Those thoughts didn't stop him from feeling forlorn, though. He'd fallen in love with Evelyn and waited patiently for her to be almost eighteen before venturing to court her. But his desire to join the military fought with his desire for his childhood friend to be his wife.

If only she'd shown an inkling of doubt about living in the community for the rest of her life, he'd have convinced her to marry him and leave with him. But since he might never come back, he wasn't sure how he could even be her boyfriend. It wasn't fair to ask her to wait for him.

A little thought came to him like a ray of hope. He could still plan to marry Evelyn. He'd never left the Amish and didn't know how life was outside the community. If his plan to join the US Army didn't succeed, he could come home and tell everyone he'd been on Rumspringa, and no one would ever have to know that he'd tried to join the Army.

Evelyn could still be his.

Theo continued studying and training with Sergeant Ethan Mills at his house for the physical fitness test. The training was grueling, but with time, he was stronger physically and was glad that he was getting closer to achieving his dreams.

Ivan decided to take out a loan and gave Theo the money for his new home. Theo opened a bank account, where he deposited the amount. However, taking out the loan put more pressure on the Glicks. They had to work harder to repay the amount and the interest. Ivan endured the extra workload, telling Theo that he'd become a responsible man. Theo didn't bother explaining that he aimed to be responsible in the military and not on a farm.

At first, he felt guilty at seeing his father work extra hard. With time, the guilt faded. He rationalized that Steven now had all the farmland instead of half while he had the monetary equivalent. That was a good deal for him and his brother. Besides, getting a loan was the best option for him and his family. His father wouldn't have to lose part of his farm, and he wouldn't have to look for who would buy his share of the inheritance.

A few weeks later, Ivan took Theo to look for land to purchase. He went along, feigning interest in the pieces of property they came across. He made the act believable as he didn't want his father to know his true intentions. He eventually picked two and told Ivan he'd choose one of them later after praying about it.

Meanwhile, he worked harder than ever at the farm, handling chores from daybreak to dusk. Elated, Ivan complimented the 'change' he'd undergone.

Steven smiled more often and told Theo he looked forward to eventually working on his own farm, but for now, he wanted to take care of their parents. That pricked Theo's conscience. He didn't want to feel guilty about his joining the military. It was a noble action, even if it meant deceiving his family in the process.

There was one person he couldn't bring himself to mislead, though—Evelyn. So, he kept his distance, acting as an acquaintance rather than a family friend who had hinted at courtship. He made sure to leave church services before she could walk up to him. When they did talk, he didn't let them veer off onto the dangerous topic of love.

He saw the disappointment and frustration etched on her face. If he were in her shoes, he'd feel the same way about someone who had shown interest and then withdrawn. But he couldn't bear to tell her the reason for his action.

He didn't know how to say, "I'm leaving the Amish for the military, and I'd like you to join me," after he had already tried to ask her, and she'd made it clear she'd never leave. He couldn't force her to decide between him and the community she loved and grew up in.

So, he danced around their Rumspringa discussion until he passed his GED and ASVAB. The only person he could celebrate his victory with was his friend, Sergeant Ethan Mills. Summer was already drawing to a close when the day for Theo to leave grew nearer. He looked forward to finally stopping the never-ending farm work and becoming part of something bigger.

For now, he had to find a reasonable excuse for leaving Unity and say goodbye to his family. He started with his father, who was in the barn taking care of a calf that had sustained an injury.

"*Daed*, I'd like to visit our relatives in Lancaster for Rumspringa before getting baptized in the church. Then I'll buy the farm and start working on it."

Ivan smiled at him. "I'll be expecting you to return soon. How long will you stay?"

"One to three months. I'll be leaving in two days."

"May your journey be blessed."

Theo smiled in return. He'd have preferred his father to bless his true journey to Army boot camp, but he'd make do with what he had gotten. Overcome with the realization that he may never see Ivan again, Theo hugged him.

"*Daed*, you're a great father, and my aim is to honor you in all that I do. Thank you for the training you've given me." It was some sort of goodbye. He hoped Ivan would chalk it up to an emotional moment.

Ivan patted his back. "You're growing into a wonderful young man, Theo. I hope you keep following the Amish way as you've chosen."

Theo nodded slightly and left, unable to bear his guilt in that moment. Now that he was about to leave Unity, Theo couldn't stand before his father and lie about following the Amish way.

The next day, he helped his mother from morning until night. He spent the day talking to her, telling her stories, and going to the local supermarket with her.

"Thank you, Theo," she said at the end of the day. "It was nice to spend the day with you. Your *daed* told me you're going to Lancaster. Will you come back?"

He nodded, choking up. "I'll try, *Maem*."

Her gaze was piercing, a trait Steven had taken after her. She kept peering into his eyes as if to read his mind until he looked away.

"I know, Theo. I'm your mother, and I know these things. I know what you're really planning. Promise that you'll come back," she said in a knowing voice, gazing into his eyes intently.

How did she know? When he spoke, his voice was small. It was difficult getting the words out of his mouth. "I'll come back. I'm going to Lancaster, *Maem*. That's all."

"You...you are?" she asked, grasping his hands with a firm grip as a confused look covered her face. "I thought you were..." She sighed, tilting her head to the side. "Are you lying to me, son?"

He swallowed and choked out the words. "No, *Maem*. It's not what you thought. You don't have to worry. I really am going to Lancaster. I promise. Please, don't worry about me. I'll be back soon."

"Oh, I'm sorry. I was wrong." She shook her head and smiled. "Well, that's such a relief. I was worried."

Theo plastered on an artificial smile as he let her believe his outright lies. She had seen right through him, but he'd convinced her otherwise. However, he didn't want her to know the truth so that she wouldn't feel obligated to tell his father and brother. Besides, he didn't want her to worry about him. He told himself it was better this way—the less she knew, the better.

He made his excuses and hurried off to his room. Despite his words, deep down in his heart, Theo wasn't sure he'd come back to Unity. So, he stayed in his room to pack a few of his belongings, not bothering to go downstairs for dinner, putting only necessities in his bag and the required documents.

He looked forward to the next day with anticipation. He'd soon be leaving his small Amish community to join the world, and he intended to achieve his dreams. He had closed his duffel bag and was about to go to sleep for the night when he heard a knock on the door. The doorknob turned, and Steven walked in with a tray of food.

"Shouldn't you be spending dinner with your family on your last day before going to Lancaster?" he asked.

"Thanks." Theo grabbed the tray, digging into the meal of chicken and dumplings.

"Don't you feel bad at all about having *Daed* take out that loan for your inheritance money?" Steven demanded with indignation as he sat down on the bed beside him.

Theo ignored the guilt bubbling up inside him. "It'll be fine."

Steven shook his head, frowning. "Do you realize the toll it's taking on him? You're leaving us to do all the extra work while you're off running around in Lancaster." Steven crossed his arms.

"I'll help when I come back," Theo lied.

Steven asked, "So, when exactly will you come back?"

"In one to three months." He figured that if he didn't pass the military training, he should come back around that time.

"Thought you'd stay longer since you love adventure."

Theo shrugged, not sure he could tell another lie. He continued enjoying the meal and wondered if the basic training food would be as delicious.

"Well," Steven said, looking around awkwardly. "Make sure you abide by our ways, read your Bible, go to church, and be good."

"You don't need to treat me like a child. I'm the older brother, remember?" Theo said, picking up his dusty Bible from his nightstand. He waved it to Steven to assure him. Dust flew off the cover, making them cough. Theo shrugged and put it in his duffel bag. "I'll read it more when I leave. Take care of *Daed* and *Maem*."

Looking conflicted, Steven hugged him. "I will. Come back soon."

Theo drove the buggy to Evelyn's house that night hours after everyone had gone to bed. He knew before leaving for her house that he couldn't look her in the face and lie to her, so he'd written a long letter hoping that she would understand when she read it. He parked the buggy a few houses from hers and walked down the lane to her house. Keeping to the side where the clothesline hung, Theo walked around to the back of the house where Evelyn's room was and climbed a tree close to her window. He folded the letter neatly and placed it between the glass panes so the wind wouldn't blow it away.

"Goodbye, Eve. I hope our paths meet someday," he said, emotion constricting his voice. He felt as though a horse had kicked him in the chest as he peered through the curtains in the window, just barely making out the form of her sitting up in her bed, reading by the light of the battery-operated lantern on her nightstand. He longed to tap on her window, but he didn't have the courage to tell her of his decision. Of course, she was up late reading when she had to wake up early the next day. That was his sweet Evelyn.

With that, he climbed down the tree and walked away into the night, his heart a mixture of sadness and elation—sadness because he was leaving his family and Eve, excitement for the new adventure he was embarking on.

When he got home, he wrote notes to Steven and his parents, snuck into their rooms, and tucked the notes in hidden places where they wouldn't find them easily.

Hopefully, it would be a while until they realized where he had truly gone.

Then he lay down on his bed, listening to owls hooting in the starlit woods. He looked around the room, committing the image to memory—clothes his mother had mended for him that he'd never gotten around to hanging in his closet, the furniture his father had made when Theo was a baby, and the simplicity of his room. He felt the softness of the bedsheets that smelled like his mother's homemade laundry soap and closed his eyes, remembering the scent of the flowers in Evelyn's garden. He knew he would miss such comforting scents and surroundings.

Before long, it was dawn. The day for Theo to go for basic training had finally arrived. He'd hired an English taxi to drive him to the Amtrak train station. They would pick up Sergeant Ethan Mills along the way.

After a quick breakfast, Theo said goodbye to his family.

His father thumped his back with pride. "Have a nice time and tell everyone we said hello."

"I will," Theo said, hugging him.

His mother hung onto Theo for a long time. She whispered in his ear, "Come back soon."

Theo's eyes filled with tears, but he quickly blinked them away as a hollow ache filled him. "I will try, *Maem*," he said, knowing it was an empty promise. Who knew how long he'd be gone?

Steven hugged him and smiled. "Don't have too much fun without us."

Theo could only nod and plaster on a fake smile. Would they miss him as much as he would miss them?

The driver arrived, and Theo quickly got in the car before he could change his mind. As the *Englisher* car drove away, Theo looked back at his family, the Glicks. They were still waving and waiting for the car to turn by the corner. He'd miss them too; his mother's comforting presence, his father's wise words and banter, his brother's dependability and readiness to help the family. He'd miss the peaceful atmosphere of the Amish community, the love he could have had with Evelyn.

He hoped the military would have the togetherness and oneness the Amish had, but he knew it wouldn't be the same. During basic training, he'd no longer have his family, the strong-knit Amish community, the church, or the familiarity of the farms and animals.

But those feelings were nothing compared to becoming an American hero. His parents would respect and admire him when the military eventually honored him for battle victories. His brother would understand why he had to leave and have an older brother to look up to. He, Theo, would have finally fulfilled his dreams. It was all he'd ever hoped for.

There was no turning back now unless he failed military training. But he'd worked hard and wasn't planning to fail. Becoming a soldier in the Army was his dream, and he would fulfill it.

Chapter Five

Evelyn woke up late that fateful day. After clearing the dinner plates and cleaning up the previous night, she'd gone to bed, put on her battery-operated light, and started reading a book. She'd become so engrossed that she'd lost all awareness of her surroundings until she turned over the last page at midnight.

When she woke up and saw the time on the battery-operated clock hanging on her wall, she'd run out of the room to find out that everyone had left the house. Luckily, it was a Friday. She didn't need to bake pastries this morning.

She got dressed and was about to open the window to air the room when she saw the piece of folded paper fluttering by the windowsill. Her heart began to beat erratically. She grinned widely. There was only one person who had ever dropped a note for her by the window. *Theo*. He'd probably come to his senses as Livia told her he would. Maybe he was now ready to talk about their relationship after avoiding mentioning it for the past few months. She hoped he had planned a time and place where they would meet.

She carefully opened the window, retrieved the paper, and began to read. The first few sentences wiped away the smile from her face. Her lips turned down into a deep frown.

Was he saying...goodbye? Had he left without her?

She sat down on her bed and started reading the letter quickly to be sure she was really seeing Theo's farewell in his handwriting.

The letter read:

Dear Eve,

The next few words might come as a surprise, but I couldn't bring myself to tell you in person.

I've always wanted to be in the Army. After seeing Sergeant Ethan Mills come back from the military when we were children in school, I wanted to become a soldier. I wanted to serve my country honorably, but as you know, it's not the Amish way. That didn't stop my burning desire to do something good for America, Eve. To help people and stop the country's enemies from doing evil against us.

I hoped you'd join me. I wanted us to get married and then leave the Amish together. But that day, when I realized you'd never leave the Amish, I couldn't take the happiness away from you. I couldn't ask you to come with me even though I want you to be my wife.

I wish that I was different. I wish that I'm the kind of man you want, but I'm not. I'll regret it if I don't try to enlist as a soldier. This might sound selfish, but I have decided to try to get into the military. If I fail basic training, I'll know that I tried. And if I pass, my dream for becoming a soldier and being of service to our country will be fulfilled. Then I hope to fulfill my dream of marrying you.

I hope you understand. I pray that we keep in touch and somehow find a way. Please understand that I still hope for the best for both of us.

I love you.

Theo.

Evelyn kept the letter beside her on the bed, hands trembling. Theo had left her. Worst of all, he'd left in the name of going off to the military. Theo had always had an insatiable appetite for experiencing new things. He hadn't spoken about his dream of joining the military in so long, she thought he'd given up on it.

She should have seen this coming.

That didn't stop the pain from hitting her like an avalanche. Tears filled her eyes and began to drop from her eyelids one after the other.

She didn't know if he'd come back. His trip wasn't just a Rumspringa outing. It was based on a decision Theo had thought about for years. Since he wasn't around and hadn't told her about his plan until he'd acted on it and left her, she didn't know how to convince him to return to Unity.

No, it was too late. There was nothing she could do to bring him back. The realization hit her like a bucket of icy water.

Looking back, his actions over the past few months became clearer. Theo had asked her about leaving the Amish to test if she'd be willing to go with him. He'd withdrawn when she rejected the idea, not because of any noble sacrifice of letting Steven court her and not hurting his brother, but because he knew she wouldn't go with him.

He'd avoided her so she wouldn't convince him to stay.

That didn't keep her from still wanting Theo. It didn't stop her from wishing he was standing before her so she could ask him the questions that burned in her heart.

Why did you leave the Amish?
Why did you leave your family?
Why did you leave me?

She fell on her bed and sobbed until no more tears could come, then she walked around and tried to do her chores in a daze. By the time her *maem*, Beverly Yoder, came back, Evelyn was sitting on the sofa and staring at the wall.

The same blue-gray eyes Evelyn saw when she looked at herself in the mirror stared at her from her mother's face. Beverly called her name, but Evelyn didn't answer. Beverly wrapped her arms around Evelyn's shoulders, giving her a warm embrace.

"Evelyn, what on earth has happened?" her mother asked soothingly.

Evelyn burst into fresh tears, feeling devastated, crushed, and hopeless. If only she'd agreed to go with him, or even better, if only she had convinced him to stay, then maybe he wouldn't be gone with no way for her to even reach him. She just wanted to think about what she'd lost.

What if Theo was injured in the military—or worse—what if he was killed? At that thought, Evelyn began sobbing into her mother's shoulder again.

Her father and brothers returned home, but she didn't register their presence. Finally, after speaking to her a few times and getting no response, they gave up trying to bring her out of her sad state.

Sometime later, Livia rushed into the living room.

"Your brothers told me something is wrong," Livia said. "What happened, Eve?"

Her brothers and father now sat at one side of the living room, talking while throwing occasional worried glances at her. She stared at Livia's concerned face, then found her voice.

"He's gone. Theo is gone," she choked out.

Livia hugged her for a long while. "He'll be back. I heard he went to Lancaster to visit his relatives."

"No, he's left for the military." She held out the letter. Suddenly realizing what Livia had told her about Theo's whereabouts, Evelyn asked, "Who told you that he went to Lancaster?"

"Steven told me he'd be leaving this morning for Lancaster," Livia told her.

Evelyn frowned.

"I saw the letter this morning. Theo lied to his brother. He could have even lied to his parents." She sighed, deflated, then whispered to herself, "I guess I'll have to wait for him."

She recalled Steven asking her to be his girlfriend and rejected the idea immediately. She'd wait for Theo before deciding what to do next. But, for now, she had to find out if he'd also lied to his parents and tell them the truth. They deserved to know their son's whereabouts.

That night, Evelyn went to bed feeling miserable. Despite how Theo had abandoned her, she only thought of what they could have had together. She never once thought about Steven in more than a friendly manner. Two brothers had shown interest in her, but the one her heart wanted had abandoned her.

How could she ever love Steven when he looked so much like his brother, the man she truly loved? Wouldn't he only remind her of Theo?

Chapter Six

The warm summer temperature suited Steven as he worked on the farm. His mother had gone to the farmers' market, and his father was out negotiating higher prices with local stores for some of their goods.

The workload would increase now that Theo had left for Lancaster, but Steven didn't mind putting in the extra work. In a few months, he'd be visiting Theo's farm and helping him out where necessary. That was what family did for each other. Before the purchase of the new farmland, he'd be content with putting in as much work as possible on his father's farm so Ivan wouldn't work extra hard.

Evelyn approached, her floral scent surrounding him. He smiled at Evelyn, then became puzzled when he saw the look on her face.

"What's wrong, Eve?" he asked.

"Theo," she said in a worried tone.

Steven brushed his hand on his pants. "Theo is away. Didn't he tell you he was leaving?" He must have decided not to tell Evelyn, which was why she hadn't come to say goodbye to him.

"Where did Theo tell you he was traveling to?" she asked, surprising him.

"He's in Lancaster," he replied. "He went to visit some of our relatives."

She shook her head. "Theo has joined the military. He's not coming back."

He chuckled in disbelief. "No. If he left the Amish, he'd have said so. Theo always talks about what he wants. He wouldn't leave without telling us."

Evelyn thrust a piece of paper at him. "He wrote this to me. Theo has joined the Army."

Steven read the note and slowly realized that she might be right. The handwriting was indeed Theo's; the letters were slanted, and each word was written as if he were in a rush to put his thoughts on paper. At the bottom was his haphazardly scrawled signature.

Yet, Steven couldn't let himself believe that his brother had written those words, made them get a loan for his inheritance, and walked around Unity pretending to be interested in buying farmland when he was secretly planning to leave to join the Army. Had he really deceived them into believing that he was visiting his relatives for Rumspringa and coming back in the winter to be baptized into the church? Steven held the note away from his body, distancing himself from the offending letter while shaking his head vigorously.

"That can't be true. Theo wouldn't do this to us. He has his faults, but he's not a liar. He would have told me that he won't be coming back," Steven said in a rush.

Evelyn's face filled with pity. "Maybe he wrote a letter to you too. He could have hidden it anywhere. He didn't give me the letter in person. He left it by my window," she explained.

On hearing that, Steven left the shed and dashed into the farmhouse. He went straight to his room to search for a note from Theo. He turned the bed over and searched the nook and crannies. He shook out the clothes on the hanger and went through the folded shirts. A neatly folded piece of paper was sticking out from the pocket of the pants he often wore to church.

His heart sinking, he picked up the paper and opened it. It was from Theo.

The note repeated most of the words in Evelyn's letter and apologized for not telling him face-to-face. It indicated where Theo had left the note to their parents and asked Steven to break the news gently to *Daed* and *Maem.*

Steven snorted. Theo could conveniently tell him to be gentle when he wasn't there to tell their parents himself. His brother had asked for money instead of land due to selfish reasons and would probably squander it away foolishly. He'd not bothered to realize how repaying the loan would take its toll on the family. Yet Theo had left them in dire circumstances because he wanted to join the Army.

How could his brother be so manipulative and selfish? How could they even be related?

Steven had the urge to crumple the paper and punch a hole through the wall. He sat down on the bed and breathed in deeply instead. After calming down, he went into his parents' room, where he found Theo's note to them, then took it to his room. They couldn't find out that way. No, he would indeed gently break it to them in person.

Steven hid the notes in a small box on his dresser and went back outside, where Evelyn was waiting for him outside. He realized the shearing needed to be finished, but there was no way he could go back to Theo's usual task after finding out what his brother had done.

He buried his grief deep inside, not letting it show before Evelyn.

"You found it?" she asked softly.

He nodded.

"I'll go now," Evelyn said. "I'm sorry that you had to find out this way."

As he watched her drive away in her buggy, Steven tried not to let the turn of events bother him. That evening, he presented the note to Ivan and Linda after dinner. He watched their faces slowly crumple into sadness and despair while reading the letter.

"He lied to us. He lied to me!" Linda cried. "I thought he was planning to go into the military, and I asked him, but he insisted my suspicions were wrong and that he really was going to Lancaster. I believed him. If I'd known he was joining the military, I would have pushed harder. I'd have convinced him to stay." Linda burst into tears; her heart shattered. Ivan held her as she sobbed, trying to comfort her, but it was no use.

"The loan was for nothing," Ivan said, anger brewing in his eyes. "What does he plan on doing with all that money?"

"It would be like him to spend it foolishly," Steven said somberly. "I'm sorry to say it, but it's true."

Tears continued to fall from Linda's eyes. Steven stood up to comfort his mother. Feeling overwhelming grief, he placed a hand on her shoulder and hugged her. She sobbed even harder. Tears pricked at Steven's eyelids, but he refused to shed a tear for the brother who had tricked them.

Theo had abandoned them. He'd left and given his family a huge debt to pay.

When his mother's crying had turned into sniffles, Steven quickly left for his room. He lay on his bed, staring at the ceiling. That night, he stayed awake, unable to sleep for a long time. Negative thoughts and emotions that he'd never felt before coursed through him. He wanted to run to wherever Theo was having basic training and ask him why he'd done this to them.

As he remembered tears flowing down his mother's cheeks, Steven knew he couldn't leave his parents at a time like this. He'd stay and help them repay the loan. Theo might have thrown the family off balance, but Steven would find a way to stabilize them.

He decided to shun Theo and never speak to him again. His brother had left without telling him or his parents, so Theo had shunned them first. Steven was simply returning the gesture. Since Theo had not been baptized into the church, they weren't obligated to shun him for leaving, but Steven chose to anyway.

The next morning, he rose early to herd the animals out of the barn to graze when he heard the bleating of sheep, his heart like a bitter rock lodged in his chest.

He came back inside to see his father in the kitchen, staring off into space.

"Good morning, *daed*," he said, burying his grief to reassure Ivan. "We'll find a way to repay the loan."

"We had hope. We thought we would see Theo's farmland and were gladly doing our best to meet the repayment terms because he had given us hope." He heaved a sigh, suddenly looking years older. "Now, my son is lost."

Steven held his father's calloused hands, imitating Ivan's usual style of encouragement. "I know that there are more things at stake now. We have a loan to pay off, which means more work with a smaller workforce, but I'll do the farm chores from morning until night every day if I have to. I'll do my best, *Daed*. We'll overcome this challenge."

"I know you'll do your best, my son. You always have, but it won't bring back the son I've lost."

Steven didn't know how to bring his father out of despair. He tried to pray, but the anger he felt against Theo was still strong. He couldn't talk to God with the negative emotions brewing inside him.

So, he hugged his father and patted his back like Ivan would have done to him. That was all he could manage, with the rage building inside him.

Chapter Seven

Theo sat on his bed, trying his best not to groan in pain from his aching, sore body. A few snickers came from the bed beside his bunk. That was the problem with sleeping in the barracks. There was no privacy.

"Amish boy," one of his fellow recruits said. "Will you disobey the drill sergeant again? If you do, it'll be even worse."

On the first day of basic training, the drill instructor had resorted to mocking him with the name Amish Boy, and the name had caught on.

Another soldier in training whispered, "The DI didn't punish him enough."

The lights went out. Theo ignored the recruits and lay down on his least painful side. Every part of his body was filled with agony, including joints and muscles he never knew he had until he started basic training.

After staying in boot camp for a few days, it became obvious that the physical exercises he'd had with Sergeant Ethan Mills were child's play. The drills stretched his endurance to its limit. As a result, his body caved in the middle of most exercises, and he barely managed to complete some.

The basic training process was humiliating. It had started with shaving the recruits' heads. The little sleep, bland food, and lack of privacy didn't help either. Drill instructors woke them up intermittently at night, and a team of recruits always surrounded Theo. The drill sergeant yelled at him at every given opportunity. After he'd told the recruits to put their bags in a line and Theo had placed his somewhere else so it would be under the shade, the sergeant had noticed and taken a special interest in him. The sergeant did not tolerate insubordination and taunted Theo regularly and punished him when he went slightly out of line.

Theo had to keep obeying his superiors, even when he felt they were wrong. He'd always thought that soldiers displayed initiative. Wasn't it such initiative that made them get medals of honor? Or could it be that the drill sergeant hated him in particular because he was Amish?

Basic training was excruciating and demeaning. If circumstances were this terrible, Theo wondered what would happen when they went on active duty. He wasn't sure he could continue. Some recruits had even started a betting pool of how long before he quit. While Theo contemplated quitting the next night, he heard a whisper from the bunk beside him. It was the same recruit that had taunted him earlier. He ignored it.

"Amish boy." The whisper was getting louder.

Theo growled furiously. "Don't call me that."

A dark-haired recruit with mischievous eyes smirked. He cocked his eyebrow in mock astonishment. "Are you not an Amish boy?"

"Not anymore," he said, ignoring the image of his family and Evelyn, the people he'd missed so much in the past few days, coming to the forefront of his mind. "I left the Amish. Besides, you say it in such a demeaning way."

Theo turned and closed his eyes. He pretended to snore so the recruit would think he was sleeping.

"Well, if you tell me your name, I won't have to call you 'Amish boy.' My name is Justin. Justin Anderson, but nobody calls me that. It's just Justin."

Theo ignored him and tried to think of his parents. How did his *maem* and *daed* feel when they found his letter? He hoped they'd understood. Things were better this way.

At least because she had stayed home, Evelyn was with her friends and family and not be alone while he was in training. Still, he had to tell her something.

"How long will you ignore me, Amish boy? At least tell me your name, and I'll give you tips on how to survive boot camp. I hope you're not planning to leave. I've placed a bet that you'll complete the basic training with this unit and join the Army. Don't give up now."

Theo's thoughts were cut short on hearing the last few sentences. "You what?"

"Talk in a whisper or the drill instructor will make you do pushups till morning."

He nodded even though Justin couldn't see him and lowered his voice. "Why would you bet on me? You don't believe I have what it takes because you keep mocking me."

"Oh," Justin said in a teasing voice. "You won't make it with that attitude, but I'm sure that if I help you, you'll become a soldier. My cousin is a soldier, so I know a few things. How about I help you, Amish Boy, to complete basic training?"

"Theo. My name is Theo."

"Theo," he said, "do we have a deal?"

"Okay," Theo said.

He didn't care about the bet, but he wondered what it would take to show the others that he could survive basic training. First, he'd show them what he was made of. Then, he'd stay and become a soldier in the US Army. It might have been impossible to pass basic training on his own, but Theo knew that with the help of a fellow recruit, he'd be able to survive and get ahead.

"Thank you," he whispered, but there was no movement from Justin. The recruit was already asleep.

Theo smiled and made up his mind to write to Evelyn. He would ask how they were all doing and promise to make their love work. He didn't know how he'd fulfill the promise, but if he could finish basic training, he'd be able to work something out with Eve. He couldn't bear the thought of her being with someone else.

Most of all, he would tell her he wanted to marry her—someday.

He wouldn't write a word to his mother, father, and Steven. He wasn't sure how they'd reacted to the letters he'd left in their rooms or how they'd feel if he sent new letters. They might even try to convince him to come back to Unity. With all the pain and punishment he'd been experiencing, if they gave him viable reasons why he should return home, he just might.

Above all, he would ask Evelyn to not tell his family that they were writing to each other. He didn't want them to be able to reach him, and he knew they would think it was scandalous for Evelyn and Theo to be exchanging intimate letters. However, he told her he would be interested in news from her about his family.

Theo wrote and mailed the letter to Evelyn the next day. He decided to put the memories of Unity at the back of his mind and concentrate on basic training. He'd come here to be a soldier in the US Army. Now that he had some support, he would try his best to fulfill that dream.

Chapter Eight

Two weeks later, Evelyn drove her buggy to her P.O. box, practically buzzing with excitement as she approached. She had given Theo the new address of her P.O. box so that her family wouldn't find his future letters in their mailbox at home.

Would she get a letter from him today? Maybe he was too busy to write to her for a while, but she couldn't help but hope.

She parked the buggy and scampered out, unlocked her box, and held back a cry of joy when she saw a letter from Theo waiting for her there. She held it lovingly, gazing at the way he'd written her name on the front before tearing it open.

Dear Evelyn,

I was thrilled to get your letter. How are you and my family doing? I will not lie and say it's easy here or that I will be coming home soon. I'll be gone for several years.

I understand if you don't want to wait for me that long, so I won't ask you to. But if you do, know that I still want to marry you.

Every day is harder than the one before, and sometimes I feel like I might just collapse from exhaustion. At first, the others made fun of me for being Amish, but I made a friend named Justin who has helped them see me differently, like one of them.

You are the only thing that keeps me going along with the hope that I will be with you again one day. When it gets hard here, I just remember your face and that walk we took by the pond when you took down your hair and let me run my fingers through it. I will never forget that day, Eve. It was when I realized I was falling in love with you.

Evelyn smiled, crushing the letter to her chest as she also remembered that day which now seemed like so long ago. He loved her then? Her heart pounded, aching for him.

I hope when I come home, we can have many days like that together, maybe even for the rest of our lives. This training has made me realize everything I took for granted when I was home and how short life is. I want to marry you one day, Eve. I hope you feel the same way about me. I promise to do everything I can to make this work between us.

Love,

Theo

After she read it as quickly as she could, she folded the letter, smiling, even though she hated to think of him facing difficulties in basic training. She pulled a pen, envelope, and stamp out of her bag and wrote him a letter in reply.

Dear Theo,

I am so sorry to hear of your struggles in basic training, but I hope it passes quickly. Your family and I are doing well, but we all miss you.

Yes, I remember that day by the pond, and it was one of the best days of my life. I knew I loved you long before then, and I want to share days like that with you too—forever. You wrote *that you want to marry me one day, and I feel the same way about you. I just hope your time away flies by so that you can come home and we can be together again.*

Stay safe.

Love,

Evelyn

Evelyn's fingers trembled as she addressed the envelope and mailed it. She then returned to her buggy, finished her errands, and drove home.

I just told him I want to marry him in a letter, she thought, shaking her head. Had she been too forward? At that moment, she didn't care. Hopefully her words would uplift him in these dark days of his life.

Once she was home in her room, she used her right index finger to smooth the surface of the paper of Theo's letter to her and looked around her room, wondering where she'd keep it. Her eyes landed on a box for storing old books, and her smile widened into a grin. It could double as a special box for keepsakes.

She held the letter in her hands like it was a precious jewel. Theo had written a letter to her from military training. He'd not forgotten her or disappeared without any further communication. Receiving the letter this morning had made her day. Knowing how he was faring made her feel connected to him; the letter was a piece of him she had to keep.

She put the letter back in its envelope and placed it in the box. Remembering the contents of the letter, she frowned. Theo hadn't been specific about when he'd be back, just that it would be at least several years. He had simply said he would find a way. That wasn't a concrete promise, but it would do at the moment. Hopefully, he'd see that he would fare better in Unity and return to her. If he didn't, she might have to be direct with him, so he'd give her a concrete answer.

She smiled sadly, wishing Theo was present instead of having to send him letters. Mere words couldn't replace their potential courtship. If only he'd been content with staying and had never left, her situation would be different. She wouldn't have to be wondering about his well-being. Instead, she'd have visited him on the farm, and they could go to Singings together in his buggy.

She shook her head, trying to dispel her wishful thoughts, and decided to visit the Glicks' farm. She'd stopped going there after telling Steven about where Theo really was and had only seen them at church. Steven's angry disposition had made his brother's action more real and shown her the impact of what he had done. She hoped they were faring better now that the shock had worn off. They had seemed alright at church.

The Glicks were busy when Evelyn drove the buggy into the farm some minutes later. Ivan, Linda, and Steven were hard at work. Evelyn was surprised to see Linda outside. Theo's mother hardly ever worked on the farm because of her frail health, allergies, and arthritis. For her to be outside doing farm work, the situation must have been dire.

Evelyn walked up to her and tried to stop her from herding a few sheep into the shed. "Go and rest, Mrs. Glick. I'll herd the sheep into the barn and help you out."

"We need to finish shearing them," Linda said in a despondent voice. "Ivan and Steven have been so busy that they haven't been able to finish it."

"I'll shear the sheep. You can go in and rest."

Linda kept walking toward the barn. "Now that Theo is gone, we're falling behind. We usually sell the fleece for a nice profit by now." Her voice was bitter, her steps measured. "If I don't take up the task, their fleece will keep growing, and I will have to..." She stopped and glanced at Evelyn. "Never mind. This is not your burden to bear, dear."

"Let me help you for a few hours before continuing with my errands," Evelyn said emphatically, holding the hand shear and trying to gently pry it away from her. "I know what to do. I've sheared the sheep with Theo several times."

Linda released the shears, her face relaxing into a smile. She gave Evelyn a bone-crushing hug for several seconds.

"Thank you." Then she went to hang out some laundry on the clothesline.

Evelyn went into the barn and began to shear the sheep. As she worked, she remembered spending time with Theo in the barn during their childhood. They laughed, played, and ran around with Steven. Theo had been outspoken, too, endearing him to her and drawing them closer over the years. After Livia, Theo was her closest friend.

Shearing the sheep without him was an uncomfortable experience. She missed him but continued removing the fleece for Linda's sake.

She'd have to take comfort in his written words. That was all she had. She thought of telling Linda about the letters but decided not to. Theo must have sent a letter to his family too. What he'd written to her was private, so she wanted to keep it a secret for him. For now, she could only hope that he'd come back soon. She loved him and was prepared to wait for him.

Though Evelyn completed the task as quickly as possible, her dress was dirty, but she didn't mind.

Steven met her in the driveway as she approached her buggy. She hadn't given him an answer yet for his request and felt too sad to talk to him now.

"Thanks, Eve," he said somberly, his usual smile gone.

"It's what you'd do for my family and me."

"Eve, I'd like to ask..."

She stiffened, knowing he wanted to bring up his request to be her boyfriend. "Let's talk about it at the Singing tonight."

He nodded and looked around at the farm wearily. "I'll be there if I finish my work on time."

Evelyn didn't want to give Steven an answer. He was clearly grieving over Theo and looking haggard. She didn't want to add to his pain by rejecting him. Instead, it made her want to stay back and not go to the Singing so he wouldn't have an opportunity to ask her.

But she'd promised Livia that she wouldn't stay home and brood all day. She would make herself seen by other potential suitors even though she had given her heart to Theo. She'd smile and sing and enjoy herself and continue living life. That should make her happier, Livia had said. However, the letter had made her the happiest she'd been since he'd left.

She went home and changed into an ankle-length navy-blue dress. She put Theo's letter in her side pocket. Just knowing it was there made her feel close to Theo.

Evelyn went to meet Livia so they'd go to the Singing together, which was being held in a house down the lane. Livia brightened when she saw Evelyn at her door.

"You look much better," she commented on Evelyn's radiant disposition as they began walking down the lane.

"I feel much better."

"So, you're getting over Theo?"

Evelyn shrugged, not wanting to mention the letter. She stopped herself from brushing her hand over the pocket with the envelope.

"I'm living with it. Theo has joined the Army, and I miss him. It makes me wonder if he'll come back. I want to wait for him. I hope he'll rejoin the Amish so we can court, but I don't know if he'll serve the rest of his life in the military. Is he worth waiting for, Livia?"

Her friend gave her a cautious look. "Do you want me to encourage you, or do you want to hear the truth?"

"Both," Evelyn said automatically.

Whenever Livia made that statement, she wanted to say something Evelyn didn't want to hear. Presently, after hearing from Theo, Evelyn needed someone to assure her that she was doing the right thing by deciding to wait for him even though he'd left the community.

"I know how much you like Theo, and I wish he had stayed. He was a good match for you. You could have courted and gotten married, but he decided to leave you. You're not even sure he'll come back. So, I suggest you suppress your memories of him and forget him. You might get to know someone else here, someone who won't abandon you but will stay by your side no matter what."

They were close to the house where the Singing would be held, so they stopped walking and continued their conversation.

"I know I should forget about Theo since he's no longer part of us, but I find it hard. Besides, I don't know what he was going through before he left. Something could have triggered his decision."

"Why are you defending someone that didn't respect you enough to tell you that he was leaving before going off to join the military? He had the opportunity to say it several times, yet he dropped off a note at your window. The note could have fallen, and you would have never seen it. Then what would have happened?"

Evelyn didn't know what to say to that. Livia's logic seemed infallible. Besides, she was grasping at straws. What if Theo changed his mind and served in the military for decades while she waited for him? Where would that leave her? By then, she'd be an old maid who had rejected possible suitors because of a man that had discarded the Amish way of life. What if he married someone else while he was away?

She shuddered at those dreary thoughts. Her heart was Theo's. It might have taken her a long time to realize it, but she had to have faith that he'd come back somehow. It was either that or give in to despair. Evelyn couldn't look at Livia when she spoke next. Her hand fiddled with the sleeve of her dress.

"I don't want to defend him. It's just that Theo is gone, and things aren't the same without him." Her voice cracked as tears filled her eyes. "Please understand, Livia. I have a strong hope that he'll come back because I don't know what else to do."

Livia's expression changed from indignation to empathy. She hugged Evelyn, letting her find comfort in her embrace.

"Oh, poor Eve. Theo's leaving must be devastating for you, as it is for his family. His parents look worn out since they lost their son. Theo left all the family responsibilities for Steven to handle. He left you devastated. You've all lost someone dear to you."

Tears fell from Evelyn's eyes. Livia wiped them away and placed her palms on Evelyn's cheeks.

"Don't cry, Eve. I just want you to understand the reality of your situation. I don't want you to keep pining for Theo when he didn't care enough to speak to you about his leaving. Sometimes it's hard to hear the truth, but only a true friend will be brave enough to tell you. You need to move on and forget about Theo, not only because he's no longer Amish but because of your emotional health. I want to see you happy again. I've missed your smile and laughter."

Evelyn blinked in an attempt to stop more tears from flowing. She couldn't tell Livia about corresponding with Theo. Her friend would convince her to stop writing letters to him.

"I miss him. I want to be with him. I…" She trailed off.

"I know, Eve. Trust me, I know. It's hard when the person you love doesn't care as much about you."

"You sound like you're speaking from experience. Do you love someone who doesn't love you back, Livia?" Evelyn asked curiously, peering at her.

Livia's face reddened as she shook her head. "No, of course not. I've just heard people say that. It's important to stay strong no matter what."

Evelyn nodded. "I'll stay strong."

They held each other's hands and walked a few steps to the house. As they were about to go in, hurried footsteps approached from behind.

"Eve."

Evelyn turned to Steven.

"Can I have a few words with you before the Singing?" he asked.

She looked at Steven. Brown curly hair, high cheekbones, and a chiseled jaw did make him incredibly handsome. However, his dark eyes gave her that piercing gaze that meant he was trying to get a read on her.

Evelyn didn't mind this time around. Following Livia's advice meant she'd need to stop nitpicking other people's attributes. It was time to forge on despite Theo's letters. She could wait for him while still leaving room for another suitor to sweep her off her feet. She could do both, couldn't she? She wasn't so sure.

Could she really be with the brother that looked so much like the only person she truly wanted?

Chapter Nine

Steven watched Evelyn carefully. Her eyelids were puffy, and her eyes were slightly red. She must have been crying a few minutes ago. He longed to hold her in his arms and comfort her.

"We have some time before the Singing. Let's go for a quick walk," he said instead. "I'd like to talk to you in private."

"I'll go inside," Livia said, giving Evelyn a knowing look before going into the house where the Singing would be held.

Steven and Evelyn walked side by side down the lane for a while. The birds chirped, insects buzzed, and a gentle breeze tickled his skin.

"I hope you're okay," he said.

Evelyn sniffed, then caught herself. "It's nothing."

"It's not nothing. It looked to me like you were crying back there."

Shaking her head, she rapidly blinked as if to stop tears from flowing down her cheeks. "I don't think you'll want to hear about it."

"You can tell me anything, Eve. Try me."

She wriggled her hands, her fingers intertwining with each other. "I... I miss Theo."

At those words, a stab of pain hit his side.

"I don't think I should miss him since he left the Amish," she rushed on. "I remember how the three of us played together when we were children. He was so mischievous, always playing pranks on us."

Steven closed his eyes, reliving those memories. Theo was his older brother. He'd looked up to him and admired his ability to persuade anybody to do what he wanted, but now Steven knew the truth. Theo twisted the truth to make people do his bidding. That was why none of them had suspected he hadn't discarded his desire to be in the military and was instead using them.

How could sweet Evelyn love someone so manipulative and deceitful?

"Steven. Steven?"

Evelyn grasped his arm. Warmth seeped into his skin from the contact. He blinked and returned to the present. She was holding both arms and shaking him.

"I'm sorry, Steven. I shouldn't have mentioned Theo. He's your brother, so you must feel the pain even more."

He felt wetness on his cheek, moving from his eye to his jaw, where a teardrop lingered. Embarrassed, Steven wiped it with the back of his hand. He hadn't come here so that Evelyn could see him crying.

Evelyn removed her hand and stepped back. "I should have known that you'd miss him more. I'm sorry."

"It's okay," he said, trying to sound calm and unaffected. "We'll get used to it."

Even then, he could see her body stiffen. Was that a slight shake of her head? He understood why Evelyn would still be in denial. If he didn't know his brother so well, he'd be thinking like her. But Steven was sure that Theo wasn't coming back soon. Theo always talked about what he wanted, went for it, and got it. That was how his brother operated.

Although Theo's actions were disheartening, Steven chose not to dwell on them. He preferred to live in the reality of the moment. Right now, he had Eve, and she needed him. He wondered how she'd feel if he reciprocated her gesture. He could pat her back, place a hand on her shoulder, or hug her, but things could either get intimate from there or get very awkward. He settled with putting his hands in his pocket to prevent them from doing anything he might regret. His words would have to suffice.

"Eve, we all miss Theo. Me, *Maem, Daed*, our neighbors, the community. But we can't deny the fact that he made his choice. So, we need to learn to live without him one day at a time."

Before he could stop himself, he pulled his hand out of his pocket as they walked and touched her arm. She turned sharply towards him. He could tell that his touch affected her, but in what way? Did her heart leap the way his did, or did she feel nothing for him?

"Please, forgive Theo," he said. "It's what I tell myself every day because I feel this rising anger towards him, especially when the workload on the farm becomes unbearable. Forgive him and face the future one step at a time. If thoughts of him become overwhelming, fill your day with work or read books to keep your mind off him." He dropped his hands, hoping his communication had been effective.

"Thank you, Steven. I appreciate that you've decided to forgive Theo and move on despite how hard it is," she said in a relieved voice. Her eyes filled with sympathy. "How are you and your parents coping on the farm? I know I don't come around to help quite as much as I used to. It's just been difficult to do so recently."

"We're managing. We've been working as hard as ever since we have less workforce. Thanks for helping us to shear the sheep. *Daed* will take the fleece to the farmer's market. Hopefully, we'll get a sizable profit."

"I saw your *maem* working on the farm. I hope everything is really okay."

"Yes, everything is fine," he said without looking at her or telling her what was really happening. But how could he tell Eve about the loan and the other sacrifices he was making because Theo left? He didn't want Evelyn to see Theo in a bad light. His brother had shocked them all with his master plan to join the Army and had deceived them with skillful maneuvering.

Steven couldn't fathom how he'd fallen for the deception. In retrospect, there had been several times when nobody knew Theo's whereabouts. Where had he been going all that time? Then there had been the overzealousness to work on the farm. His brother had acted in his usual manner when he wanted something from the family—doing whatever they wanted, working on the farm from dawn until dark. He'd continued in that manner even after getting the inheritance money and picking the supposed farmland he wanted to buy.

Steven should have known that there had been something else his brother wanted. If Steven had bothered to investigate instead of trusting blindly, he would have found out about the join-the-military plot. He could have noticed that Theo was planning to leave the Amish and spoken to their parents, who would have stopped him.

A ball of fury settled in his chest. "God, help me," he muttered under his breath, not wanting the anger to worsen.

"What did you say?" Evelyn asked.

"Nothing."

He resumed walking, Evelyn walking alongside him. It was better to live in the moment than discuss or think about Theo. Things were simpler that way. He focused on Eve and her lovely features, her skin glowing in the pink light of the sunset. The sun's final rays illuminated her heart-shaped face and a few strands of golden curls that had fallen from her *kapp*. Their feet crunched in the dirt as they made their way down the lane. He didn't care if they missed the entire Singing, and she didn't seem to mind either.

"Tell me a story from one of your books," he said, wanting to hear her sweet voice while basking in her floral scent. It would lighten the mood, making both of them feel better.

She spoke, her face lighting up. Her smile made his lips turn up, and his eyes softened. As she talked about her perception of the recent book she was reading, he forgot all the work he'd left on the farm and how he'd have to take care of his parents without Theo.

He remembered why he'd fallen in love with Evelyn in the first place. She mended his heart without even knowing it, though she hadn't replied to his request to be her boyfriend yet. He just figured she wasn't ready to get involved in anything romantic. When she'd been climbing into her buggy earlier that day, he'd had the urge to be with her. She'd saved him from an awkward moment by suggesting the Singing. Right here, Steven saw another opportunity to ask to court her.

Still, a dark memory surfaced in his mind—Theo's first letter to Evelyn, which had stated that he wanted to marry her. Did that mean that they'd started courting? Had Theo been so cruel that he'd left his girlfriend to join the military and had asked her to wait for him? In light of recent events, Steven wouldn't be surprised if his brother had acted out of the norm.

He took one long look at Evelyn. Theo wasn't coming back, so Steven felt he could ask to marry her. But then, Eve was grieving hard. Her smiles still had a hint of sadness. He wasn't sure she'd say yes to him if he asked her to be his girlfriend at this time. Maybe she needed more time to let go of his brother.

Besides, he had to take care of his family. There was too much work on the farm because of the extra resources needed to pay the loan. Plus, he didn't have the financial capacity to take a wife now. That would require building his own house to raise his family. Even if he did, his parents needed him.

He had to focus on helping his parents and paying back the loan. After that, he'd ask Evelyn to court him. Maybe by then, she'd have forgotten about Theo, and it might be easier for her to say yes.

By the time they'd finished their walk and gone back to the Singing, Steven could hear voices singing a hymn from the *Ausbund.* It was a harmonic blend that made him want to go in and join them, but he had to go home and rest so he could wake up before dawn the next day. Besides, he'd already had a beautiful time with Evelyn.

He told Evelyn goodbye with a grin on his face, wishing they'd have more moments like this. Then he went to his buggy and rode back home. The cool night air was comforting as he rode past houses and made his way to the farm. He hummed the song along the way, no longer feeling tired or weary. The anger against Theo that still burned in his chest was of little consequence. Right now, he concentrated on thoughts of lovely Evelyn.

Steven now had something to look forward to.

Chapter Ten

Theo put his hand around his shirt collar in an attempt to free his neck from the tie's constraint. For the first time in his life, he was wearing a shirt with a collar and necktie.

After he and Justin had become friends, he'd gone on to finish basic combat training, pass his physical fitness test, and complete advanced individual training. Presently, he was on a short break for a few days. Then he would be deployed with his unit.

Unfortunately, he'd not gone back to Unity despite spending several months away in training. He hadn't mustered the courage to go back to his family. His parents would either refuse to speak to him or try to convince him to stay in Unity. He couldn't bear either scenario. He was duty-bound to the Army and the United States of America.

Instead, Theo had gone to Justin's house. When he saw the way his friend's mother looked at her son, he'd wished that his *daed* would look at him that way just once. It didn't matter that he'd finally achieved what he'd always wanted. It wasn't the same if Ivan didn't look at him with pride and acceptance.

Becoming a national hero was great, but it was nothing when your family didn't value what you had done. Besides, being in the military didn't bring the fulfillment he'd envisioned. The physical and mental training had hardened him, making him tougher, less hot-headed, and more responsible. He had new comrades who were now like his brothers, but once in a while, Theo wondered if he'd made the right choice by leaving the Amish.

The grueling training had been the opposite of his father's gentle reprimands and Steven's accusations. He missed his mother and Evelyn, especially Eve. The letters made him long for her more. In a way, writing to each other had made his love for her grow.

But he knew he'd soon be in combat, and Eve didn't deserve the kind of man he would become. He'd chosen a path that could lead to not marrying her. Still, he wasn't ready to let go of her.

"Amish boy," Justin called jokingly from the living room, and the term of endearment no longer offended Theo. "Are you coming?"

In the bathroom, Theo ignored him and put on jeans and a t-shirt, then went into the living room.

"Where are we going?" he said, then turned to Justin's mother. "Good evening, Mrs. Anderson."

The woman beamed. "Come back quickly, boys."

Her attention was on her son as she spoke, her eyes filled with adulation. They said their goodbyes and got into a car, Justin in the driver's seat and Theo in the passenger's seat.

"Where are we going, Justin?" Theo repeated.

"It's a secret," his friend answered cryptically.

"This is one of your jokes, isn't it?" Theo asked.

"Nah. Not a joke in any way. If I had told you where we were headed, you wouldn't have gotten into the car, Amish boy. Besides, it's a Friday night. Where else would we be going?"

They drove until they reached a nightclub. Even from the parking lot, the music was blaring. Theo thought the sound would deafen his ears. The dazzling multicolored lights from the building made him want to close his eyes. He definitely wouldn't have entered the car if he'd known Justin had planned to drag him to a club. He crossed his arms over his chest.

"Turn the car around. Let's go back." He couldn't bring himself to say, 'go back *home.*' No matter how welcoming Justin's mother was, his home was with his own family—Ivan, Linda, Steven, and Evelyn.

Justin laughed. "Why? Have you lost all the backbone you grew in basic training?"

Theo assessed the situation. Justin was determined to take him into that club. Theo didn't know how to drive. It wasn't like the Amish in Unity drove cars, but how hard could it be? All he needed to do was turn the key in the ignition to move the car. It's not like there was a horse to hitch up to the front.

He reached out to take the car key.

Justin snatched the key and put it in his pocket. "No, no, no. That's not going to happen. You're not going to crash this car tonight. You don't even have a license. So now, you've got two options. You can walk into the club with me and have a good time. Or you can sit in the car, and I'll keep telling the story of how you chickened out from entering a club for the rest of your military career."

Before Theo fully processed his thoughts, he opened the door, got out, and slammed it shut. Justin was taking the joke too far. His friend didn't understand the Amish way of life. He didn't want to accept that Theo was different and usually found ways to ridicule him. Although they'd bonded because of a simple bet, Theo had expected that they would grow beyond that.

Justin was grinning. "I knew you'd come around. Let's get into the club."

"I'm taking a taxi. You can tell *your* comrades whatever you want," he said in a bitter tone and started walking out of the parking lot.

There was stunned silence for a few seconds. Then he heard hurried footsteps behind him before Justin's hand landed on his shoulders.

"Hey, man. You don't need to get upset. We can leave if you want."

Theo turned, his gaze hardened. "I explained the Amish way of life to you during boot camp, and you've made it your duty to mock me about it. You knew who I was before you decided to become my friend. Even though I left the Amish, I still honor many of the rules I grew up with. Take it or you leave it."

"Fine." Justin raised his hands in surrender. "I get it. No more Amish jokes."

Theo arched his eyebrows.

"I'll stop. But come on, if you left the Amish to join the Army, then experience life to the fullest. Just go into the club with me. You don't need to dance or drink if you don't want to, although drinking would help you forget things."

Theo peered at Justin. What would it hurt to have a few drinks? He wouldn't let himself get drunk.

"Come on. There's nothing wrong with a few drinks, Theo," Justin persisted. "I'll be with you the whole time."

His friend's expression seemed sincere, so against his better judgment, he walked to the nightclub. He'd just take a few drinks, which would help him forget his family and Evelyn. When he got in, he focused on the bar, not the scantily clad ladies. He ordered a few drinks and paid for him and Justin. Justin danced with several women while Theo surveyed the scene with a drink in his hand. Staying here was better than brooding about Evelyn and his family.

Some ladies with sultry eyes walked up to him. Soon, he was buying drinks for them and letting them drink on his tab. As a brunette flirted with him, he found himself flirting back. Then remembering Evelyn's pink lips and golden hair that cascaded down the back, he suddenly made an excuse and walked away.

He would keep everything under control. He'd learned that sort of discipline in the Army, after all.

Theo woke up the next morning with a hangover. His head felt like it was splitting in two, and the sunlight streaming in from the room window was too bright. Guilt slammed into him as he recalled how he'd kept drinking the previous night until he became drunk.

Usually, he prayed and found peace when he acted out of character. But that had been long ago. He brought out his Bible from his bag, opened it, and looked at the pages. He closed his eyes and tried to talk to God, yet he couldn't bring himself to pray. What would he say after not speaking to Him for months? He felt like a fraud. Eventually, he picked up a letter he'd received from Evelyn before the end of his training.

The letter soothed him. It also implored him to come back home, but that was something he couldn't do. He should write back and tell Evelyn the truth—he wasn't returning anytime soon. Yet he needed her comforting words. He'd just avoid the topic of going back home.

The short break ended, and Theo and Justin were deployed overseas. They served in the same unit and eventually went to war. As infantry soldiers on the field, they used different defense and warfare tactics.

There was a heart-pounding fear that always accompanied Theo in battle. The first day he saw an enemy soldier die, a wall of revulsion, guilt, and remorse slammed into him. Soldiering was a serious business that involved life and death, and he was responsible for taking away some of those lives.

Theo's smiles became few and far between, and he wore a solemn expression most times. He didn't want to take lives, so he subverted instructions from his commanding officer that would involve killing while making it look like he was proactive in battle. One day, an enemy soldier shot him. A military doctor gave him battlefield treatment and then took him to the infirmary.

Justin barged into the infirmary later on, furious.

"What is wrong with you?" he demanded. "Do you want to die out there before you stop being stubborn? You need to start following instructions." Justin's hands and voice were trembling even though he was shouting, showing how much he cared for his friend.

"I obeyed orders. I was executing the commander's intent even though I didn't follow instructions to the T," he said, wincing in pain. "And I have paid for it dearly. I'm in big trouble."

"Not only that, but if you had obeyed, you wouldn't have gotten injured or put the team in jeopardy. Think about all you did in the field today, Theo, and imagine a situation where you'd actually followed the commander's orders correctly. Then consider if things would have turned out differently."

When Justin left, Theo thought about the battle that had led to his injury. He imagined what he could have done better as opposed to following his superior's command. In all the scenarios he brought up, he realized that the commanding officer's orders kept the troop safe.

Luckily, the injury wasn't lethal. The bullet went clean through near his clavicle, but if it had been a few inches in another direction, it could have hit his heart or carotid artery in his neck, which would have killed him.

Coming that close to death made him realize he might not ever make it home. He might never see Evelyn again.

And he knew how unfair it was of him to expect her to wait for him, but he still wanted her in his life. Desperately. Even if it was only through letters. Just knowing she was thinking of him warmed his heart.

The idea that he had to comply and obey orders, including killing, sunk in. He knew this might eventually become his reality, but he'd avoided it as long as possible. Sticking to his Amish beliefs of nonviolence was causing more harm than good on the frontlines. He knew he had to put it behind him and start following orders. That was why he was here, wasn't it?

The experience made Theo think about his family. So that day, he wrote to Evelyn, but he didn't mention his injury—he didn't want her to worry.

Dear Evelyn,

Lately I have been thinking of my family even more. Will you take care of them for me? Will you check in on them and help them with the farm when you can? I worry about them, but if I knew you were helping them, it would ease my mind. Please help them be strong. I hope they don't worry about me.

I miss you, Evelyn. You are my angel. When I come home, we will put all of this behind us.

Love,

Theo

If he couldn't be there for his family, maybe Evelyn's help would suffice.

Chapter Eleven

Steven covered his shivering parents with the blanket. Ivan and Linda had been sick for a while now. Despite the warmer spring temperature, they'd not gotten better.

"God, please heal them," he prayed as he returned to clean the barn.

After his parents fell ill, they'd fallen behind on the loan repayments. Steven feared the bank would seize their property; he couldn't afford to slack in his duties if he wanted to make the next payment. So, he'd be holding a livestock auction the next day. Hopefully, the money would be enough to pay the debt. If not, they'd have to sell off part of their land, which was something no one wanted to do.

Usually, the Amish community would help in situations like this, but Steven didn't want to ask for help. He could do it all himself and prove to his parents that he would take care of them and the farm. He still had a lot to do. His family needed the money desperately.

He would hold a livestock auction and ensure the barn was immaculately clean, so anyone purchasing an animal would see how well the animals had been taken care of. Still, Steven wasn't sure he could complete the tasks before the sale.

He shut his eyes again to pray.

"God, please," he said before a fit of familiar rage rose within him. His *daed* and *maem* wouldn't be ill if they had not taken out the loan. Instead, they had to bear the grief of Theo leaving the Amish, joining the military, and repaying a loan that was taking a toll on them, both physically and mentally.

Steven found himself mucking the stalls with more force than necessary. He should concentrate on getting his parents out of their predicament instead of thinking of a brother who was long gone, but he couldn't stop the pain welling up inside him. He needed to ask the bishop for help. The sage advice he'd get would help stop the anger.

After several futile attempts, he stopped trying to say a more elaborate prayer. He worked from morning till evening, till his bones and feet ached, yet he ended up only cleaning a small section of the barn and feeding the animals. He sat down on a stool and stared into the distance.

"Steven," a voice called from the open barn door.

He jerked his head towards the entrance. Evelyn's brothers, Joe and Elijah, were standing by the door.

"We heard you need some help," Joe said. "I've told some *Englishers* I know to buy from you at the livestock auction."

"We'll help you with the sale," Elijah said. "And if that's not enough, we'll get more help."

Steven breathed a sigh of relief, a wobbling smile on his face. The Amish community was his family, and they'd come to help when he needed them the most. He showed each person what to do.

Steven let his hopes rise again. If everything worked out as planned, adding chickens and eggs to their farm produce would be beneficial. He started whistling as they worked into the night.

"Are you going to the Singing today? You haven't been in a while," Joe said suddenly, making him remember that there was a Singing that night. He'd missed several and had stopped keeping count of when the events were held.

He shook his head. "I have to take care of *Daed* and *Maem*."

"Well, we're here, and Livia's *maem* has volunteered to stay with them. You can go. Besides, Evelyn will be at the Singing," he said with a knowing smile.

Steven looked around. His friends were hard at work, using battery-operated lanterns in the barn. It had been a while since the sky darkened outside. The Singing must have started, but he could still go if he hurried.

"Thank you all so much for coming. It's late. You should all go home," he said, not wanting to leave before them.

Once they were gone, he rushed out of the barn, changed his clothes in his room, hitched up the buggy, and drove to the house where the Singing was held.

He hoped to see Evelyn and talk to her. Except for when she had visited his sick parents recently, they hadn't spoken privately for months. Though he did see her at church and community events, he hadn't been able to ask her about what was happening in her life lately.

It wouldn't be far-fetched to wonder if Evelyn had caught the eye of another suitor. She was beautiful, gentle, and would make a good wife. If his family got to the point where they paid the loan regularly without problems, he would ask to court her.

He rode on, oblivious to the environment. By the time he arrived, he realized that he couldn't hear voices singing or talking. A few people were milling around the door, but

Evelyn and her friends were not there. They'd probably gone home after the Singing ended.

He shouldn't have let himself hope so much. The Amish community taking care of his parents and volunteering to work on the farm was already enough help. If he'd simply enjoyed what God had sent him, he wouldn't have had to think about Evelyn.

Steven bowed his head and walked back to his buggy. Then he rode home, sullen.

Chapter Twelve

Theo has not been communicating with his family since he left for the Army, so he doesn't know his parents were sick, Evelyn thought as she read Theo's letter in her room.

Dear Evelyn,

As you know, basic training was so much more difficult than I ever imagined, but I made a friend there who helped me through it. We've been deployed together overseas, and I've now seen the horrors of war. I've seen comrades die.

Sometimes I just close my eyes and picture your face.

I miss the sounds of the animals on the farm, the wheat swaying in the breeze, and Maem's *food. Oh, how I miss her food. The food here keeps us alive, but it's nothing like what my mother makes.*

Most of all, I miss my family, and I miss you. I wish I could be with you more than anything. I didn't realize I would miss you so much it hurts. I also didn't realize that combat would be this brutal and horrifying. It isn't the glorious experience I imagined, but I'm getting through it.

Evelyn sighed, wiping a tear away, but not before another one fell and stained the paper.

You haven't told my family we've been writing, have you? I'm sorry I had to ask you not to tell, but I know they would think it's inappropriate for us to keep in touch, and there are so many things I just can't bear to tell them. Please check up on them and let me know they are well.

You are my heart, Evelyn. I can't wait for the day when I can return and hold you in my arms.

While I wish you had come with me so we could be married by now, maybe even with children, I know I wouldn't have been able to see you very much and you would have been alone most of the time. I wouldn't have wanted that for you.

Evelyn paused, a sob shaking her shoulders. What would her life be like if she had gone with him and married him? Would she have been happy? She missed him so much, she could hardly bear it. Was he safe? What if he got injured—or worse?

Please, Lord, keep Theo safe, she prayed, just like she did dozens of times every day.

Evelyn had suspected Theo wouldn't write to his family, and it was so difficult for her not to tell them he was writing to her. If they knew he was writing to her but not them, she feared it may break their hearts.

She paused, listening for the sound of footsteps. She didn't want anyone to barge into her room. Her brothers, Elijah and Joe, were each getting married that weekend. The house was filled with numerous visitors. Relatives from other states and communities had come to help with the wedding preparations.

Although Evelyn had picked up the letter at her P.O. box the previous day while running some errands with a relative, there had been no time to read it until now, not with people milling around in the house and the loss of privacy as a result. She certainly didn't want the news of her reading Theo's letters to spread. She'd finally gotten her chance today when there was nobody in her room to ask her whom she was corresponding with.

After reading the paragraph where he asked her to check up on his family and tell him how they were doing, she realized the depth of Theo's negligence. If he wasn't writing to them, it only meant that they didn't know where he was or what had become of him. They couldn't write to him either.

She wondered if she should give them his forwarding address but dismissed the idea the next second. Although she still went to the Glick's farm, she didn't go there as often as she had before. Since Theo was no longer around, it wasn't easy seeing reminders of him. Besides, she couldn't tell them that she'd been receiving letters from Theo all this time without telling them some of the contents of his letters and where he was now.

The sound of laughter and footsteps drifted up from the stairs. Evelyn shot up from her chair and thrust the letter into her box for old books where she now kept all Theo's letters between their pages. She dumped the box in the wardrobe just as her room door opened to reveal Livia.

Livia gave her a concerned look, glancing at the box. "Sorry I came late. I had to help my *maem* out with a few things. Your *maem* needs you in the kitchen."

Evelyn gave her a polite smile and pulled her hair into a bun, avoiding Livia's eyes. She picked up her *kapp* from the table and tied it on her head.

"I just need a few minutes," she mumbled. "I'll come to the kitchen soon."

"Okay. See you down there." Livia left the room.

Evelyn dashed to the box, retrieved the letter, and quickly finished reading it. She wrote back:

Dear Theo,

I wish you could tell me where you are. I worry about you so much, but I pray for you even more. I'm glad you've made a friend, but it makes me sick to think of what you're experiencing so far away from here.

No, I haven't told your parents we've been writing, though I wish I could. You probably don't know this, but your parents have been sick. By the time you get this, maybe they will be better, though it could take them weeks to fully recover and regain their strength.

Before they got sick, your parents were working long hours, and your mother was trying to help with the extra farm work. Now that they're sick, Steven has to work even more, and he's too busy and too tired to attend Singings.

It would mean the world to them if you wrote to them, I'm sure. Won't you consider writing to them? They must be so worried about you. I know you might think they wouldn't write back, but you won't know unless you try.

I miss you so much, and I wish I could hold you in my arms, too.

A tear fell from her eye and stained the paper as she finished writing the letter. She put it back into the box, hiding the box in the wardrobe before leaving the room. She'd have to mail it later.

By the time she walked down the stairs, Livia was helping prepare the wedding meal in the kitchen with other women who had come to help. Evelyn looked around but couldn't find Theo's family. Ivan and Linda had just recovered from another illness; she didn't expect them to be present.

Steven was probably hard at work on the farm. Her earliest memories of Steven were of him working hard on the farm to impress his father, while Theo only wanted to run around and play. Steven's sense of responsibility had only increased when Theo had left, and she didn't think it would stop anytime soon.

Still, she dreamed of Theo surprising her and coming home to see her. He'd cock his head to the side and give her a mischievous look. His smile would light up her heart. She'd smile back, and they'd take walks along fields filled with wildflowers.

"Eve, what are you thinking about?" Livia asked, interrupting her thoughts.

She blinked, trying to come up with what to say.

Her friend's eyes lit up. "Who is he? And what were you hiding in your closet?"

Evelyn looked around, aghast. Did anybody hear the questions? Luckily, people weren't paying attention to Evelyn. She shook her head, trying to give Livia a signal that she wasn't comfortable talking in the kitchen. From the corner of her eye, she could see her mother, Beverly, peering intently at her. Had she overheard?

"There is no one," she whispered, leaning in closer to her friend.

A grin formed on her friend's face. "There's definitely someone. You were acting strangely in your room."

She ignored Livia as her mother called her over and gave her some instructions on baking pastries. Her mother finished with a meaningful, "We'll talk later."

"Yes, *Maem*," Evelyn mumbled, shifting her weight from side to side uncomfortably.

Evelyn rushed to her friends, thoroughly embarrassed. She enlisted their help in making the dough and pretended she'd not been the center of attention the last few minutes, but she knew Livia wouldn't let go of her assumption. There was no new person in her life. It was only Theo. Talking about him would displease her friend, so Evelyn chose to tell only part of the truth.

"I was thinking about the Glicks when you came into the room," she said to Livia. "I'll be going to the farm later. I wonder how they're doing without Theo. I hope Ivan and Linda are healthy. Steven needs to stop working so hard, too."

Livia snorted. "He doesn't have a choice, does he? He's the only son available at the moment. Sometimes, I wonder how he copes. He's quite strong, taking care of his parents and managing the farm alone. Some other men wouldn't work as hard if they were in his position. And those that can might have fallen ill or given up by now."

Evelyn nodded and measured the flour. She gave Livia several eggs to beat.

"I wanted to bring this up later, but since we're talking about the Glick's, I guess this is the right time," Livia said.

Evelyn paused and looked up.

"I think we should help Steven. I've been going over to the farm, but I can't do it all the time. There's a lot of work to do at my house," Livia explained. "The help I've given him so far has made little impact, but if we take turns, we'll make his work less burdensome."

Evelyn baked twice a week, so she wasn't as busy as the other two. If she agreed to Livia's plan, she'd be the one going to the Glick's farm most times.

"Eve, let's do this to help Steven and his parents," Livia said in a pleading tone.

Evelyn contemplated her friend's request. Helping the Glick's seemed to be important to Livia. Or was it? Maybe Livia was trying to push her towards Steven. Otherwise, why would she bring up a scenario where Evelyn would be with Theo's brother most days?

But then Theo had asked Evelyn to take care of his family. If she visited the farm frequently, she'd make sure Linda wouldn't come outside to work. She'd take flowers to them and help prepare food if Theo's mother was too weak and didn't want anyone to know. Then the farmhouse would be filled with warmth, glorious scents, smiles, and happiness. She'd write all about it to Theo, too. He'd see why he should come back to her and help his ailing parents. That way, she'd be fulfilling Theo and Livia's wishes.

"I'll help the Glicks, but you have to help when you can," she said, wagging a finger at her friend.

Livia hugged her, making sure not to soil her dress with dough-covered hands. "Thanks, Eve. This will make Steven admire you even more."

"What? No," she exclaimed. "Why did you say that? I have no feelings for him."

"But he asked you to be his girlfriend, and you were considering him. You might change your mind," Livia said, smiling mischievously.

She shook her head vigorously. "I won't. You know that I don't see him that way. He's like a brother to me."

Evelyn suddenly realized that her surroundings were quiet. The spoon scraping the pot a few seconds ago had stopped. The voices of the women talking in the kitchen had gone silent. This time around, it wasn't only her mother peering at her; every woman in the kitchen was looking at her.

Her cheeks heated up in embarrassment.

"Never mind," she said and quickly looked down.

She kept at her task, not daring to look up until the kitchen was noisy, the cast iron pan on the woodstove sizzled, the pastries were fully baked, and the sweet and savory fragrances of the food made her stomach rumble.

They soon moved on to other discussions. Evelyn didn't talk about her romantic longings for Theo. She spoke of her desire to buy a box for keepsakes. In a way, she expressed her desire for Theo since the box would hold his letters.

After the meal preparation, Evelyn's mother took her to her bedroom. Her mother's graying brown hair was tied up in a bun underneath her *kapp*, her blue-gray eyes displayed wisdom, and her advice had helped in numerous situations.

"Let's sit," Beverly said, and they both sat on the bed.

Evelyn gulped and placed her hands on her thighs, willing them to remain flat and not fidget. Her mother couldn't notice her nervousness, or she'd pry out the secret about Theo with skillful questions.

"Can you tell me what that was about?" Beverly asked. "Who were you and your friend talking about in the kitchen?"

"We were talking about...Steven," Evelyn replied, deciding to pick the more appropriate answer. She'd been keeping Theo's letters a secret for so long that she could no longer confide in her mother.

"Are you lying to me, Evelyn?"

A few breaths later, she squeaked out, "No, *Maem*."

She didn't mention Theo despite her mother repeatedly asking who Livia had been referring to or what she was hiding in her box.

After a while, Beverly put an arm around her shoulder. "Eve, you know I want the best for you, and I won't condemn you, but I can't help you if you're keeping secrets from me."

Evelyn remained silent and stared at her hands in her lap.

Her mother sighed. "Maybe you want to sort things out on your own, but remember that I'm always here whenever you need me. Don't forget all I've taught you; always pray and seek God's guidance."

"Yes, *Maem*." Evelyn stood up and walked to the door.

"One more thing," Beverly said, causing Evelyn to stop by the door. "You should consider saying yes to Steven if he is the one who is interested in you. Sometimes, what you want is already in front of you."

Evelyn hastily left the room, blushing furiously.

All through that day and the next, she thought about her mother's words and how Livia had convinced her to help Steven. She wouldn't put it past her friend to be matchmaking. And Beverly seemed to have joined in even though she didn't know the one Evelyn loved was Theo, Steven's brother.

After Elijah and Joe each had their own weddings, they moved to their respective homes. The house was quiet, and Evelyn had less laundry and cooking, but with her brothers gone, she felt more lonely.

Nevertheless, Evelyn and Livia went to the Glick's farm regularly. Except for greeting the family, Evelyn avoided talking to Steven as much as possible. She was here to help because of Theo and not to fraternize or be involved in Livia's hidden plans.

With time, she came to appreciate Steven's quiet strength and his attentiveness and willingness to help selflessly. She wished Theo had a little of those character traits. If he did, she wouldn't be in this predicament.

She also noticed that whenever she and Livia were at the Glicks' farm together, her friend spent her time talking to Steven instead of working. Occasionally, they glanced at her and smiled. The action irked her. Frowning, she pointedly ignored them and focused on her tasks, trying to put the state of the farm to memory so she could write to Theo about it later.

One day, Livia walked up to her while she was herding the sheep.

"What's the matter, Eve? You've been frowning a lot since we started helping Steven out," she said, getting straight to the point in her usual manner.

"Well, you've been talking a lot lately instead of working," Evelyn replied, not bothering to hide her displeasure.

"Steven is glad that we've been helping him. He said I should thank you."

Evelyn turned her head towards Steven, who was grinning at them. It had been a long time since she'd seen a smile on his face.

"Okay," she said and went to Steven.

His eyes lit up. His countenance was different—open and warm, yet calm. Something about the way he looked at her reminded her of Theo. The gaze was similar and made her feel warm inside.

"Thank you for coming out to help me. I appreciate it," he said.

He has long eyelashes, just like Theo's, she thought.

"You don't know how much this means to me," he continued.

But she wasn't listening to him anymore. Her eyes went to his arm, which seemed to be fighting to stay by his side. He reached towards her and then drew back stiffly. Did he want to hold her hand but was stopping himself for propriety's sake?

By the time he'd finished speaking, she smiled widely to hide the fact that she hadn't heard what he said. Something had changed in Steven. The set of his shoulders was different—not only had he become stronger physically, but his character had also grown. The way he talked to her and her friends was different too. He stood taller and spoke with more authority, just like his brother. Taking care of his parents and managing the farm alone seemed to have made him a better man.

He had become more confident. More appealing.

After that day, Evelyn found herself going back to the farm again and again. She told herself that she was helping Theo, taking care of his family. But sometimes, she admitted to herself that she went to see the brother who was developing attractive qualities.

On her birthday, Steven bought her a trilogy of novels—three wonderfully thick hardcovers she kept running her fingers over. He also brought her a big pot of flowers. They were sitting on the porch drinking lemonade, taking a break from farm work, when he presented the gifts to her.

"The roses are artificial; I hope you don't mind. I wanted them to be beside you in your room all year long." He touched a soft pink rose petal as he spoke.

"Pink roses remind me of your kindness, but I wish they were all different colors like your personality. The orange roses would remind me of when you light up a room without making any effort. The purple roses would depict your calmness, and the reds would remind me of your selflessness. Some of the suggestions you've made since you started helping me out on the farm have helped greatly," he explained in a low voice.

She looked away, surprised by his surprisingly sweet words. "Steven, I had no idea you were so poetic," she murmured. Who was this man who had replaced the little boy she'd grown up with?

"You make me want to be poetic." He shrugged, giving her a sheepish grin. Unable to maintain eye contact, she shyly looked away, noticing two birds chirping and circling each other. Ivan was in the barn while Linda was preparing a mouth-watering lunch that Evelyn looked forward to eating with them. Despite the sound of the animals and the gentle breeze on her skin reminding her that they weren't alone, she felt like those two birds, talking with Steven in an intimate conversation. She touched the petal, feeling its softness between her fingers.

"Thank you," she said shyly.

"I haven't finished yet," he said, going into the farmhouse and bringing out a dark blue box. It was a perfect size for keeping the letters from Theo.

Oh, the irony, she thought.

"What's this for?" she asked, surprised.

"Well, I thought you'd like a box for keepsakes. If not, you can keep the books I bought for you in it."

But she hadn't told Steven that she needed a box. How had he known? Then it dawned on her. Only Livia knew she wanted this specific trilogy, and she'd told her friend about wanting a box. Livia must have told Steven about her wishes.

Her heart pounded as she glanced from the gifts to Steven. The books, flowers, and the box weren't simply given to make her happy. Steven wanted her to love him back, and Livia was in on his plan.

She was standing a hair's breadth from him, almost touching him. Not knowing when she'd moved so close, she hastily stepped back and shook her head. A smile appeared on Steven's face. Evelyn looked away. She loved Theo, not his brother. Truly, she did. This moment, whatever it was, was only because she was missing her soldier.

If only he'd stayed.

She focused on Steven. "Thank you for the gifts. I appreciate your kindness and the thoughtfulness you put into getting me all these on my birthday. I'd like to invite you to dinner at my house this evening," she said in a formal tone.

Don't accept the invitation. Please don't. I only asked out of courtesy.

Scrutinizing her expression, he smiled. "Actually, I would love to come over to your house tonight. I'll be glad to see your *maem* and *daed,* and Elijah and Joe. Oh, I forgot they each got married. Will your brothers be at the dinner?"

"Yes." If Theo had stayed in Unity, maybe she'd have gotten married at the same time as her brothers had.

"How are their wives doing?"

"They're doing fine. It's early, but I think Elijah and his wife will be welcoming a baby soon. I want to have lots of children someday," she squeaked out, realizing that she had just sent him a message she had not intended to. Had Steven read into her comment?

He just looked at her and smiled, and Evelyn sighed. *Why did I blurt that out?*

Theo was no longer Amish. Everybody had moved on, including his brother. But she was hanging on to their love, a love that was no longer as pure and strong as it used to be. Memories of spending time with him brought a mixture of exhilaration and heartache, a pain that seemed to be growing daily.

"Eve," Steven said, stepping closer. He had the scent of the fields and barn on him, but it comforted her. "What's wrong?"

She wanted to lean in, let him embrace her, and clean the tears that had begun to run down her cheeks. But she couldn't. She wouldn't.

She grabbed the pot and lifted it up, using it as a shield between them. Trying to balance the pot of flowers, the book, and the box, she scurried to her buggy.

"Let me help you carry the gifts," Steven said, walking briskly beside her.

She ignored him and managed to put them in the buggy. She climbed in.

"Eve, you've only been here for a short while. Why don't you stay for lunch?"

"I have to go home and help my mother with the chores." She stared at him boldly, daring him to refute the excuse. "I'm sorry. I can't stay."

"See you tonight," he said, stretching his hand to remove a piece of hay that had stuck on the sleeve of her dress.

She jerked back and picked off the offending piece of hay herself. A hurtful look crossed his face. She smiled to placate him. "See you tonight."

The dinner turned out to be a bigger affair than Evelyn had anticipated. She'd also invited Livia. Before Steven arrived, Evelyn took Livia to her room and showed her all the gifts he'd given her. She twirled around in excitement and hugged her friend.

"Thank you, Livia. I've wanted to buy these things but never got around to it, and you convinced Steven to get them for me, didn't you?" She paused. "You're quiet. Why are you quiet?"

"I didn't know...I didn't think he'd buy them so quickly. Steven is a good man."

"Yes, he is nice. But he's not..." She trailed off, not wanting to say the words: *he's not Theo*.

Her eyes went to her closet where the box filled with letters was hidden. Theo was corresponding with only her and no one else, not even his family. That must mean something. He loved her and would come back to marry her after his short stint in the military. She had to hold on to that hope despite the widening pain that ricocheted in her chest whenever she thought of him.

She looked forward to discovering the man he'd grown into when he came back. He'd be more responsible, wiser.

It didn't matter that he was far away today and Steven was here enticing her with his gifts. She had only one mission on the farm—to help take care of Theo's family as he'd pleaded with her to do.

After dinner, she avoided taking a walk with Steven by giving the excuse of tiredness. When everyone had gone back to their houses and rooms, she brought out all Theo's letters and read them chronologically, from the first to the last. Then she folded them and arranged them neatly in the box Steven had gotten for her.

Somehow, Theo's letters in Steven's box looked wrong. It felt wrong. But she stubbornly left them there. She told herself that each time she looked at the box, she would remember the letters and why she'd gotten the gift in the first place. Because she'd been helping Theo, the one she loved, even though he wasn't here to talk to her and wish her happy birthday in person, give her gifts, or take her for walks in the meadow as he had in the past.

She sat down at her desk and began to write another letter to him. That would help her sort out her emotions. Because no matter how much she tried to give excuses for Theo or remind herself of the vast ocean of love she had for him, the ache was still there.

Steven had somehow entrenched himself in her emotions. It didn't help that he was almost a carbon copy of his brother and had started displaying some of his behavioral tendencies.

Things had gotten a lot more complicated.

Chapter Thirteen

Theo got Evelyn's letter about how his parents were sick, but he still didn't write to them. He knew they'd only try to convince him to come home, so he couldn't bring himself to do it.

As time passed, Theo had become a good soldier. He obeyed his commanding officer without question, obliterating the enemy. But with each bullet, a little more of his Amish self died because he was snuffing out the lives of fellow human beings instead of forgiving.

He now understood why his father had been adamant about the violence in the military. As a soldier who had been on the frontlines several times, he was an example of how killing changed a man. He could see the whirlpool of hardness in his eyes when he looked in the mirror. The guilt in his heart had become a bottomless pit. No amount of reasoning, not even the idea that he was honoring his country, could assuage it.

The military had tainted him. That knowledge made his correspondence with Evelyn difficult.

She had become his lifeline, offering comfort when he needed it, calming and soothing him, enthusiastically responding to his tales, telling him about her life and all that happened in the Amish community. She'd helped take care of the farm and his parents when they were ill.

He loved her. Sweet, innocent Eve. He still wanted to marry her, to be her husband, and for her to be his wife. He had not been able to have a girlfriend because of her, though many women had shown interest in him. His comrades called him a prude, but Theo didn't mind. Evelyn was his love.

And with each stain he got on his heart from the violence of war, his heart seemed to move farther away from her even though he clutched Eve's letters in his hands.

Days turned to weeks, weeks turned to months, and months turned to years as he was promoted in the Army.

One day, Theo couldn't open the envelope he clenched. He was twenty-four years old now.

Evelyn's letter would make him smile and calm him, he knew it. But she'd also talk about when they'd marry and live as husband and wife. She would paint grand pictures of him coming back to the Amish as a hero and how proud his family would be.

Oh, how he wished she was right.

He wasn't coming back to the Amish. His soul was too dark for the peaceful community he'd grown up in. It was time to let go of Evelyn.

When he eventually opened the envelope and read the letter, his suspicions were confirmed. He wrote a reply before he chickened out, each stroke of his pen a laborious walk up a lonely mountain.

Dear Eve,

I read your letter. Thank you for sending yet another one.

You asked me to give you a definite date when I'll be coming back to Unity, and I've made my decision. I'm sorry, my darling, but I won't be coming back to Unity. I won't be writing to my family. There's no point. They will only try to convince me to come home if they do write back.

I have given my body and life to the military. I am a soldier honoring my country on the frontlines.

And that's all I can ever be now.

I'll be moving to a new base a week from the date on this letter.

I hope you understand that I had no choice. Even when I retire, I don't think I'll come back to Unity, Maine or rejoin the Amish community even then.

I need to let you go. It wasn't fair of me to let you wait for me for so long, and I'm sorry. I never should have been so selfish. You deserve to find someone who will make you happy.

Forget me. Have a wonderful life, my Evelyn.

Your Theo.

It wasn't his usual writing style, but that was all he could come up with. For several weeks, he couldn't post the letter to Evelyn. When he eventually settled into his new military base, he posted it. He made sure not to send a forwarding address. That meant he wouldn't receive any more letters from her.

After posting the letter, Theo locked himself in the bathroom. A gut-wrenching moan emanated from him.

Loss. Pain. That was all he felt.

But it was better to let Evelyn go, wasn't it?

His job as an infantry soldier had tainted him, and he wouldn't spread that to his Eve. He couldn't let himself ruin her life by making her wait for him even more than she already had. Had she passed up potential suitors because of him, men who could have loved her better than he could have?

He loved Evelyn. Unfortunately, it was a love that couldn't be shared because she was too sweet and innocent for his dark heart.

And he'd been a selfish fool to ask her to wait for him.

Chapter Fourteen

Steven opened his eyes in the morning and smiled. It was going to be a sunny day. He felt joy welling up inside him because of his plans for the day. He left the farmhouse, opened the barn, and began to herd the animals outside.

Several years ago, his parents had been ill and had the loan repayment tied around their necks like a chain. But now, they'd paid off the loan and had farmhands working for them. The business was thriving. Best of all, Ivan and Linda were no longer falling ill. Today, he'd tell them of his intention to court Evelyn.

Once the farmhands arrived, he delegated responsibilities to them and went in to eat breakfast. After the meal, he waited for Ivan and Linda to sit at their usual spot where they preferred to spend time together talking almost every morning. He gave them a progress report of the farm, then told them about his intended courtship.

"*Daed, Maem*, I intend to ask Evelyn to be my girlfriend today. I want to marry her."

There was silence in the living room, the type Steven wasn't comfortable with. He noticed the sickness had taken its toll on his parents. Though they had recovered, they'd lost weight and looked weaker than their usual selves.

"Steven, my son," Linda said gently. "Did you know that Theo wanted to marry Evelyn before he left?"

"*Maem*, I only knew about Theo's desire to marry Evelyn after he joined the Army. But Theo left six years ago. Besides, I wanted to marry Eve, too. I've waited for her to let him go. I also wanted to complete the loan repayment before getting married to lessen the financial burden of raising a family and paying off debt at the same time. That's why I worked so hard to repay the loan back early and sold part of the land."

"And you did an excellent job, son, and we appreciate everything you did to repay the loan early. You made the right decision by selling part of our land. It was necessary," his father said.

"Of course, son, but what if Evelyn says no? Will you let go of your desire to marry her and focus on other women who might be a better fit for you?" Linda asked.

Steven shook his head. Nobody else was a better fit. "I've waited for Evelyn to develop feelings for me, and I think she has let go of Theo and has feelings for me now. Otherwise, I wouldn't have decided to ask her."

"You haven't answered my question," Linda said with a slight knowing smile.

"I just hope she says yes."

Linda nodded and became silent.

"My concern is not about Evelyn. She has a good head on her shoulders and knows how to make her own decisions," Ivan said, leaning forward. "I'm more worried about what your actions will cause. Evelyn and Theo had something before he joined the Army. I can't tell if it was mere attraction or if they'd begun courting, but it was quite strong. Every time Evelyn talks to me, she mentions Theo, and her countenance brightens. She might be still in love with your brother. If I'm right, that could lead to disastrous consequences if you court or get married."

Steven shifted uncomfortably in his seat. He didn't like how the conversation was focusing on Theo, even though he was miles away in an unknown location. Why should his brother influence any decision the household was making? He could feel anger rising up in him. He quickly recited the scripture Bishop Byler had given him for such situations in his head: "Do not be quick-tempered, for anger is the friend of fools."

"I don't think they ever courted. Before Theo left, we were both Evelyn's friends and we all acted like siblings."

"What if they did court?" Ivan asked.

Steven breathed in and out slowly to remain calm. "I'll ask her if she and Theo were courting. We'll sort out whatever occurred between them when she agrees to my proposal. I think she'll say she never courted Theo."

Ivan didn't look satisfied. "You should find another lady to court, Steven. My gut tells me that Evelyn isn't for you. Theo would be so devastated."

Steven chuckled bitterly.

"*Daed*, how are Theo's feelings important in this situation? He abandoned her. I didn't know he had romantic feelings for her until he left. He never told me about dating Eve or wanting to court her. And even if he'd wanted to, he chose to leave her here and join the military. He made a choice and did not respect her feelings." The intensity of his emotions made him stand up and pace the living room. "Let's not forget that he left us with a loan repayment, and you fell ill when you worked so hard to catch up. He's been away for six years, *daed*, not six days. There has been no word from him since then, so he doesn't plan to come back. Would it be wrong to court the lady I've always loved just because Theo wanted her briefly before deciding to abandon us?"

Ivan stood up and walked slowly to him, then placed his hands on his shoulders. Panting with rage, Steven stared at his father.

"I'm only trying to avoid problems in the future. I don't want you to get hurt." Ivan paused and looked into the distance as if searching for how to put his thoughts into words. "Do you remember when we discussed several methods that would help us repay the loan quickly?"

Steven nodded.

"That's the same thought process. You're thinking about everything that could go right between you and Evelyn, and I'm thinking about everything that could go wrong. It's only when we bring up these scenarios that we can tackle them and make sure we come out with the best solution."

"*Daed*," he said, anguished, "I love Evelyn. If Theo had mentioned that he loved her or wanted to marry her when he was still here, I'd have tried my best not to pay attention to what I felt for her. But he didn't. And by the time I found out, it was already too late. My feelings were too deep, and Theo had left. Besides, he's not coming back."

"He's not likely to come back soon," his father corrected, "but he might."

Steven snorted but didn't argue. Ivan was keeping hope alive; it was what a loving father would do. But Steven preferred to judge things based on reality. Theo had no intentions of coming back to the Amish, or he'd have written a letter to them. When his parents had fallen ill, Steven had gone to Sergeant Ethan Mills to find out his brother's whereabouts. He'd sent a letter to the forwarding address Ethan had given him but had gotten no response. Steven later found out that the address was wrong. The sergeant didn't know Theo's location or wasn't telling them what he knew.

"Alright," Steven said. "Let's say he comes back ten years from now or whenever he retires. He'll probably be married with children. Should I then sacrifice my love for Evelyn for someone who didn't even date her at best or abandoned her at worst?"

His father was silent. His mother watched both of them intently.

"*Daed, Maem,*" he said, hoping they'd agree with him.

"Just ask Evelyn if they ever courted and if she still loves him," Ivan replied. "Her answer should determine what you do next. If she still loves him, I advise you to look for someone else to marry. But if they didn't, you're free to make your choice. It would be out of respect for your brother."

Steven felt a note of apprehension. He'd never bothered to ask Evelyn about that letter where Theo had talked about his intention to marry her. What if they'd actually started courting? He reassured himself that they hadn't and put the thought out of his mind.

Ivan motioned to Steven to sit down. They walked back to the sofa together. "I have something important to tell you, too."

He paused, and Linda continued where he stopped.

"We've been severely ill a few times, and you took care of us relentlessly. Your diligence and loyalty are admirable."

Steven beamed under the praise of his mother. He loved how his parents were a team, knowing how to handle a conversation together effortlessly.

"You've also expanded the farm and made it more profitable," Ivan chimed in. "You've added a larger greenhouse and chickens, and you were largely responsible for paying off the loan completely even though we barely made the payments a few times."

He bowed his head respectfully. "Thank you, *Daed*. Thank you, *Maem*. Your words mean so much to me."

"But," his father said, raising up one index finger, "I had different ideas. I still don't agree with some of the things you did, but I have to accept that it worked out well in the end. You've made me a proud father with your responsible and mature behavior. I wouldn't wish for a better son."

Steven's smile widened. He couldn't control it. After Evelyn and Livia came to help, Steven realized that the farm was much more productive whenever they were around. He'd gone ahead to hire farm hands afterward. At first, it had seemed a costly decision. But once the loan had been fully repaid, he used any extra money to expand the farm operations. Then productivity and profits skyrocketed.

"I'd like to take all the praise for myself, but I can't. Evelyn was very helpful. She organized her friends to help us out when everything seemed dire. She also made suggestions that improved our farm operations. These are part of the reason why I want to marry her," Steven explained.

"Hmm. Just be careful; that's all I'm saying. It's better you avoid future problems before they become too big to handle."

"Thank you, *Daed*."

"The farm is yours, Steven," Ivan told him, beaming.

"Really?" Steven asked, eyes wide, barely believing what he was hearing.

"You've earned the ownership with the loan repayment. But since I have to strengthen my bones to become as agile as I used to be, I'll be coming back to work now that I'm completely well. We'll work together as partners, and your ideas will be implemented. I will let you take the lead."

Steven's chest puffed up, and he sat straighter, elated. "I've missed working alongside you and can't wait for you to come back."

Finally, he thought, *Daed recognizes all my hard work.*

Steven was no longer living in his brother's shadow or only acknowledged after Ivan had first recognized Theo. In a way, Theo's leaving had helped him. Steven didn't have to live in his shadow anymore. His brother's absence had forced him to grow and develop. He'd been able to take care of the farm and head off some problems that would have been much worse later on.

He'd proven his worth to Ivan. He'd made his father proud. That mattered most.

That evening, Steven knocked on Evelyn's front door awkwardly. He brushed his hands over his shirt and adjusted his stance nervously. He was once again about to finally ask the girl of his dreams to court him.

The door opened, and Evelyn stood in front of him. She was radiant as always. Her eyes lit up at the sight of him, and she gave him an angelic smile.

"Can I come in?" he asked, reciting what he planned to say in his head.

"Oh, yes. Sorry for keeping you waiting."

She moved aside, and he walked into the living room. The house was quiet. Books littered the chairs, so Steven moved some aside and sat down.

"Sorry for the mess," Evelyn said, looking around as if she was seeing her own living room for the first time. She wriggled her hands. "I've been reading a lot lately to occupy myself. I've not been keeping the books on the shelf, and now I need to alphabetize them."

"It's okay," Steven said, brushing her apology off with a smile. "Everyone knows you're a bookworm. Where's your *daed* and *maem*?"

"They're in their room. They decided to go to bed early."

He nodded, wondering how to start.

"What are you doing here, Steven? This is an unexpected visit. Not that you can't visit whenever you like, but..." she trailed off.

That was his opening. Where should he begin? What should he tell her? His fingers trembled slightly. He leaned forward, eagerly.

"Eve, you look beautiful as always."

The battery-operated lanterns illuminated her face. He could see a blush forming on her cheeks as she looked down. The color complimented her eyes. "You shouldn't say such things."

"I've had feelings for you for so long, and I believe you've developed feelings for me also."

She blinked, her expression unreadable. His heart pounded as he continued on.

"I want to be with you for the rest of my life. I want to court you and eventually marry you. We can have as many children as you want," he blurted, wringing his hands. Maybe he should have waited to add on that last part.

She stiffened. Maybe she wasn't as ready as he'd thought. She could be scared of getting married.

"Alright, we don't have to get engaged immediately. But...will you be my girlfriend, Eve?"

A heavy silence descended on the room. Evelyn looked everywhere else but at him.

"I...I..." She pinched her nose. "I can't be your girlfriend."

"Why?" he asked softly. "Don't you have feelings for me?"

Her eyes went back to him, and desire pooled in her eyes. Then she looked away. "It doesn't matter if I have feelings for you or not. I can't."

Steven thought for a while. Had he asked her too late? Maybe some other suitor had asked for her hand, and she'd agreed. He should have asked her when she was still coming to the farm.

"Did someone else ask you to marry him?" he asked.

She shook her head.

"Then what is it, Eve? Tell me."

"I want to get a job at a store. Since my brothers have gotten married and I've stopped coming to the farm every day, there's hardly anything to do around here. *Daed* and *Maem* don't eat much. I've reread my books so many times. I want to do something with my life and be useful and productive, so I want to get a job. I don't like being idle."

Steven's first inclination was to ask how her getting a job would affect if they courted or not, but he thought about her desire and realized there was more to it. Evelyn was solely focused on getting a job. It could only mean that she wanted to be independent and wasn't planning on getting married.

"Alright," he said. "I can employ you on the farm. That will take care of your wanting a job. Besides, once we get married, you won't need to work."

"No, no," she exclaimed. "I can't work at your farm. I want to find a job working somewhere else."

He crossed his hands over his chest. "What's the real reason why you're getting a job? I know you're not telling me everything."

She sighed. "I don't want to talk about it, Steven. Basically, I want to be a valuable member of the community, and I don't want to be a burden to anyone." She leaned forward. "Please help me get a job."

Although Steven had expected Eve to say yes, he'd never thought it would be easy. He would help her as best as he could, but he first needed to soften her decision.

"I'll help you."

She smiled, and he felt his stomach lurch with excitement.

"Please, Eve. Just give me one more chance. Think about what I said and give me your answer a few days from now. If you're still not comfortable with getting married to me, I'll back off and never talk about it again."

"Okay, I'll think about it," she said, clasping her hands together.

A ball of hope settled in Steven's chest. If everything went as planned, soon Evelyn would realize how much he loved her and would love him back.

Chapter Fifteen

The next day, tears fell from Evelyn's eyes as she read Theo's letter over and over again. The words he'd written telling her he wasn't coming home pierced her heart.

When she hadn't accepted Steven's request to be his girlfriend, it was because she had still been hoping Theo would come home. Now she knew that would never happen.

She closed her eyes, shuddering at the prospect of no longer being with Theo. Although they'd only been exchanging letters, her love for him had blossomed. They'd grown closer and spoken freely. She knew more about Theo and felt her heart was intertwined with his despite being miles apart.

But now, he'd severed the connection between them because she'd insisted on knowing the exact time he'd come back to Unity. He was living a different life, which he apparently loved more than her.

Yet, she believed she had made the right decision by insisting he gave her a definite answer about returning. She'd waited for six years and had rejected potential suitors all because of Theo.

She started reading his letters again, from the very first letter he'd attached to her window pane, wondering where she'd gone wrong. She'd had delusions about his choosing her over his stay in the military. After reading a few letters, she couldn't continue. She closed the box and pushed it aside.

Light reflected on the dark blue box, and the memory of Steven giving it to her as a gift resurfaced—his smile, the way he'd looked at her, and her fluttering stomach. Could that feeling develop into the kind of love she had for Theo? Would it be right to date and marry Theo's brother?

What she felt for Steven wasn't as strong as what she had for Theo. Sometimes, she thought it was infatuation. At other times, she felt she truly liked him.

But then, Theo was moving from base to base and would get married someday while she was here alone. Since he wasn't coming back and they'd never courted, it didn't really matter if she pursued her feelings in that area. There was no harm in accepting his brother's proposal since she'd never see him again. If she had agreed to be Steven's girlfriend years ago, she would be his wife by now, and they would probably even have children at this point.

Theo had made his choice; it was time she made hers. But did she truly love Steven? Did she want to spend the rest of her life with him, or would she spend her days wishing he was his brother?

A knock on the front door interrupted her thoughts. Remembering that she and Livia had planned to buy groceries, she raced down the stairs and opened the door. It had been a while since they'd gone out together. On their way to the supermarket, they caught up on recent local events and what was going on in each other's lives. Livia told many stories that uplifted Evelyn's spirit. The buggy's rhythmic sound was comforting as the horse's hooves clip-clopped down the road.

This was what Evelyn had been missing since her brothers had both gotten married and she had stopped helping Steven at the farm—someone to frequently spend time with. Her mother usually went out to visit her friends. Evelyn was glad her mother now had the time to do so, but it often left her alone. Her father worked more, so she also saw him less and less.

Now that she was with Livia, she felt much better. If she courted Steven, she'd spend lots of time with him and not have to be alone. She decided to tell her friend about her decision.

"Steven asked to court me," she said, holding the horse reins a little too tightly as the buggy rumbled down the road.

Livia was silent for a few seconds. "What was your reply?" she asked, her face devoid of any emotional display.

"I told him no at first, and then agreed to think about it, and I'm going to accept him as my boyfriend today."

"Do you love him, Eve?"

She sighed. "I don't know, Livia. I like him more than I used to, though. I think I have feelings for him, but I'm not sure it's love." At the confused look on Livia's face, she defended how she felt. Evelyn continued, "It's just that he's been so good to me that I find myself responding to his display of love. Besides, I'm getting older. I've always wanted to marry at a young age. I know I'm only twenty-four, but if I keep rejecting all my suitors, I might not have anyone to marry by the time I'm thirty."

"I understand your concerns, Eve, but love is an important foundation for any marriage. Do you think you can ever love him?" Livia asked.

She nodded, hoping she was right. "I already have feelings for him. If we cultivate it, it can grow into love."

Livia sighed. "Well, if Steven makes you happy and you desire to marry him, you should go ahead. But Eve, I also know how you felt about Theo, and you haven't gone on any dates since he's left. It won't be fair to Steven if you're courting him and thinking of his brother."

Evelyn felt a pang of guilt. Part of her reason for wanting to date Steven was because of his similarity to Theo. It was a start. But with time, she could like him fully for himself.

"Before you marry him, you must completely let go of Theo to be fair to Steven. That won't happen on its own just from marrying Steven. Once you've done that and you and Steven are together, you'll have to give him every bit of your heart. You'll be happier that way, and your marriage will be better."

With that, Livia became silent, and Evelyn pondered her friend's advice. She would have to make sure Steven didn't know that she still thought of Theo. She'd ensure they had a long courtship, so by the time they got married, she'd have put her first love out of her mind.

To show appreciation for how he had paid attention to her for so long, Evelyn knitted mittens for Steven. A few days later, he took her to a bookstore.

"I have a surprise for you," he said, smiling.

She looked around, wondering if he wanted to buy a book for her and had brought her here to pick out a novel.

"I got a job for you here. The store manager buys fresh milk from our farm. When you said you wanted a job, I remembered your love for books and asked him if he was hiring, and he was," he said.

She beamed, feeling joy overwhelm her. She'd wanted the job at first so she could get away from the house, but getting a job in a bookstore was her chance to read and discover new authors. She hadn't bought books for so long and had been rereading her collections. If she was careful, she could read all the books lined on the store's shelves without soiling any of them.

"Thank you so much," she gushed.

"You're welcome, always."

After they'd spoken to the store manager and Evelyn had been briefed on the job details, she took Steven to the coffee shop. It was time to accept his proposal.

She had chosen the coffee shop because it was the first place he'd asked her to be his girlfriend. Since then, he hadn't pressured her into making a decision but had waited patiently. That was a great feat of strength she admired. Besides, Steven was a loyal and hardworking man. He'd stayed with his family and taken care of his parents. He would be a good husband, and they'd have wonderful children together.

The hot cocoa they'd ordered arrived, the aroma from the mug was pleasant. It was familiar and reliable, just like the man sitting in front of her. Evelyn took a sip and closed her eyes. When she opened them, Steven was drinking from his cup and staring at her.

She brought out the mittens she'd packaged in a colorful patterned wrapping paper and handed them over to him, smiling shyly.

"I made these for you."

Steven beamed. "Thanks, Eve."

"I know it's not much, but I want to say thank you for your help and care. You've always been there. Thank you for the gifts you've given me and for the job."

One eyebrow arched. "You made mittens to thank me for the job before I got a job for you?"

Heat spread on her cheeks. "Not really. I wasn't thinking about the job when I made them, but I knew you'd help me out. That was why I asked you."

He nodded.

"I've thought about your request like you asked me to, and I have an answer ready. I brought you to this coffee shop because it was the first place you asked me to be your girlfriend."

He became more alert immediately, keeping the mug on the table. "Before you continue, can I ask you a few questions?"

"*Ja*, go ahead."

"Did you have feelings for Theo?"

Evelyn's eyes widened, then she composed herself and nodded. "Yes, I did."

"Were you ever his girlfriend, or did you court him?"

"Steven! If I courted Theo, you would have known because we would have informed our parents."

"Couples often date in secret, too. You know that. Please, humor me and give me an answer."

Evelyn sighed. She hadn't expected this interrogation. "We didn't date or court. Before he left, we went for walks in the meadow and a few other places, but we were only friends then."

Steven visibly relaxed. "Do you still have feelings for him? Do you love him?" he asked gently.

She scratched a sudden itch that had appeared on her forearm and looked away. "I...um...I... The answer is complicated."

"Please explain."

She rubbed her temple with her finger. Even if she escaped these questions now, they'd come up later. She braced herself and decided to pour out her heart to him.

"I'm going to be upfront with you. I had a crush on Theo when we were teenagers, but nothing came of it. We didn't date, and we certainly didn't court. He left. Now, I've realized that there's only one person for me." She stared into his eyes as she spoke the next sentence. "You've been there for me, and you love me, and I want to spend the rest of my life with you. That's why I'm saying yes today."

"Thanks, Eve," Steven said and took her hand, stroking the back of her hand.

Evelyn didn't feel anything substantial when he touched her hand, just a little warmth. She wondered how she would feel if his brother was stroking her hand in the same way. Were they just that—feelings? Or did it mean something more?

She hadn't been able to tell Steven about the letters because the pain of Theo's message was still raw. She wasn't sure she'd be able to tell him since Theo hadn't sent any letters to his family.

Evelyn had only one option, to burn the letters. She wouldn't see Theo ever again. Then she'd be able to put keepsakes of Steven in her box. She'd keep showing him love until every inch of her heart was his to care for and cherish.

Maybe once she did that and finally let go of Theo completely along with all hope that he would come back, then there would be enough room in her heart for her to fall in love with Steven.

She withdrew her hand. As much as she was willing to put in work to make their relationship blossom, she wasn't comfortable with such a bold show of affection, especially in public. What if someone they knew saw them?

"I don't want to rush things; I'd like us to have a long courtship," she said. "If we do, everything will fall in place naturally, and we'll have a good marriage."

His eyes dimmed. He nodded stiffly and smiled. "I understand. Let's not rush things."

Evelyn told herself that she'd made the right choice. Accepting Steven's offer of courtship was for the best, and having a long courtship would ensure that she loved him by the time they became husband and wife.

After the date, late that night she burned all Theo's letters in the woodstove and vowed not to write to him again. As she watched them disintegrate in the flames, her heart wrenched and she sobbed softly, but she knew this was necessary. Tomorrow she would cancel her P.O. box.

He clearly doesn't love me. Steven loves me, she thought.

Theo had not left a forwarding address, so it might be easier to keep to her vow. And even if he had a change of heart and contacted her, she wouldn't reply.

Evelyn and Steven became boyfriend and girlfriend, and Evelyn tried to love him as best as she could. Somewhere in her heart, she didn't feel the spark she'd felt with Theo. Yet, she persevered as the months passed by.

Chapter Sixteen

Theo could feel his body tossing and turning on the bed as he gripped the sheets with his hands. His eyes shot open, heart pounding with fear. He'd had a nightmare.

Just then, pain lanced through his torso. He gritted his teeth, remembering where he lay. The walls and bedsheets were white. He was hooked to equipment that monitored his vitals. He'd been in the hospital for several months and wasn't sure when he'd be discharged. The bland, white walls always made him think of how he was no longer pure-hearted. Such thoughts reinforced his bad dreams.

Just like every other time he'd woken up from a nightmare, the details of the mission that gave him this life-threatening injury came back to him.

He'd been injured again.

It had been a simple enough mission, but things got bad quickly. His comrades in arms got pinned by enemy fire. Theo had tried his best to cover them. It was only when he'd heard a shot, a body thumping to the ground, and a groan that sounded eerily like Justin's that he'd felt overwhelming dread. He'd sprinted to his friend to find a bullet lodged in his body. As he pulled his friend and other comrades to safety, Theo was shot brutally in the abdomen and leg. He'd fallen down and banged his head on a boulder, then everything went black.

He didn't know how he'd been rescued from the battlefield or how he had survived this long. He had been unconscious for several months due to a traumatic head injury then had awakened. Luckily, the bullets hadn't punctured any organs, arteries or bones. His leg wouldn't be amputated, but he'd need to go through physical therapy.

Even though Theo had miraculously survived, Justin had passed away, his closest friend from the Army. Theo tried not to think about him as much as possible. He was a friend that had turned into a brother.

Now that he'd had a near-death experience and Justin was no longer around, Theo missed his family more than ever. He had not spoken to *Daed, Maem*, and Steven for several years. He'd cut off all communication from Evelyn. He'd let go of his Amish beliefs, everything his parents had taught him.

The disappointment he felt was familiar. It was quickly turning to unending despair. There was only one thing he could do—pray. Although Theo had stopped talking to God for years, he began to pray:

"God," he said softly while staring solemnly at the blank hospital walls, "I'm sorry I have been avoiding praying to you. Please give me the strength to carry on despite the injuries I sustained. Help me to accept Justin's death."

His voice broke when he mentioned his friend's name. He paused for a few seconds, composed himself, then said, "May the peace of God that surpasses all understanding guard my heart. Lord, help me to reconcile with my family."

With that, he closed his eyes and drifted off into a dreamless sleep.

After a few weeks, Theo was discharged from the hospital and stayed in a veteran's shelter to recuperate until he found an apartment. He had to keep on undergoing physical therapy while using crutches. With the limited movement of his leg, he couldn't go back to active duty. There was hardly anything to fill up his day. Instead, he had persistent negative emotions and more nightmares. He frequently had flashbacks of the battle that had left him in his present state, wondering if he could have done anything differently to change the outcome.

Theo was honorably discharged from the military with a purple heart medal. He'd served his country as he'd set out to, yet all he felt was deep dissatisfaction. He had pursued one goal at the expense of embracing his family, the Amish community, and getting married to the love of his life. He'd seen many horrors during his time on the frontlines. Theo knew he was scarred. He'd known it for a long time, but he'd had Justin then.

Now, all he could think of was Evelyn's hopeful gaze, his father's calm advice, his mother's soft words, and his brother persistently working on the farm. He missed everything about his family, even the arguments he'd had with Ivan. He'd take the arguments they had any day over the dreary, lonely existence he was presently in.

He wanted to rejoin the Amish, go to church, participate in the Singings, and marry Eve. But he'd been away for so long; he wasn't the same anymore. Would the Amish accept him back? If the bishop would baptize him and they accepted him, he could become a member of the church. But that didn't mean everyone in the community would accept him with open arms.

He knew he had hurt Evelyn and wondered if she'd accept him back. She could have moved on, or she might even be married. But what if she wasn't?

With time, one thing became clear to Theo. Wallowing in depression wouldn't help him find out. He'd been experiencing Post Traumatic Stress Disorder ever since the accident. The therapy was helping. His newfound zeal for reading the Bible and praying to God made him feel better. But his guilt kept mounting, and the PTSD remained like a monster clawing in the back of his mind.

He could rejoin the Amish despite being tainted, as long as he repented. Maybe they'd help him. He'd need to find out if Evelyn was still single, if she would forgive and accept him.

He was filled with hope for the first time in a long time. Just the mere thoughts of home—the smell of his mother's stew on the woodstove, the breeze blowing the curtains in his bedroom window, and the softness of the grass in the yard brought him comfort.

Hopefully, he'd truly get better—mentally and physically—when he rejoined the Amish.

Once Theo had made up his mind, it didn't take long for him to wrap up his affairs. He sold his belongings, visited Justin's mother to say goodbye and tell her of her son's bravery, then left for Unity.

"I have a surprise for you," Steven said as they walked along the pond in Unity—the same pond Theo had mentioned in his first letter to her, saying this was where he'd first realized he was falling in love with her.

Now Steven had brought her here in his buggy as a surprise, and he had something to show her here. As they walked along the edge of the water with the grass swaying around them in the breeze, it didn't quite feel right. This place was meant for her and Theo, and being here with Steven felt wrong in a way.

Theo isn't here now, and no one knows when he might be coming back—if at all, she told herself as they walked. *Steven is here, and he cares about me. It's time to let go of the past.*

"Here it is," Steven said, gesturing toward a blanket spread out on the grass and a picnic basket.

"You set up a picnic for us?" she asked, smiling. "How sweet."

"Well, I wanted it to be special," he said, blushing as they made their way over and sat down.

Special? Why? She gulped. Was he about to ask her what she thought he might ask her?

Steven took her hands in his as they sat on the blanket. "Evelyn, you are everything. I love you, and I have for a long time. I want to spend the rest of my life with you. Will you marry me?"

Evelyn's throat went dry, and while she was filled with comfort as he held her hands in his, a small part of her also wanted to pull away and tell him she had to keep waiting for Theo.

I've waited for him long enough. It's been years. I can't keep on waiting and wasting my life away. Steven is a good man, and I do love him, she told herself. *Even if I don't feel butterflies like I did when Theo held my hand, that doesn't mean anything. I still love him.*

In her mind, all she could see was Theo's face, but she pushed the image away. Her thoughts raced, but she ignored them all.

"Yes, Steven, I will marry you," she said confidently, and he grinned.

"Oh, Evelyn, you've made me the happiest man in the world!" Not wanting to be improper by giving her a kiss on the lips before marriage, he leaned forward and kissed her cheek.

"Let's eat," he said, opening the basket and handing her a sandwich. "We have so much to talk about."

She took the sandwich and smiled, but once again, Theo's face filled her mind.

Lord, help me forget him, she asked God. *It was just a silly infatuation. I love Steven now, and it's time I let go of his brother and move on with my life.*

The moment the car he'd hired drove into Unity, Theo was overcome with nostalgia. The Amish boys and girls playing in the fields reminded him of his childhood. The squeaking wheels of a passing buggy made him turn to the side, wishing he could come out of the car and climb into the buggy. The warm summer climate was welcoming. Trees and flowers blossomed, and pigeons flapped their wings in flight.

Theo felt a burden lift from his heart. He was back home. Then a wave of anxiety hit him. How would his family react to him coming back? What about Evelyn? He wasn't sure he could bear it if she was already married or if she rejected him.

He was moving past Evelyn's house when he made a spur-of-the-moment decision to visit her and asked the driver to stop. A horse was hitched to their buggy in the yard. Maybe he could get a ride home later. He came out of the vehicle and placed the crutch under the arm opposite the weaker leg. The driver removed the luggage from the trunk, then Theo paid him, and he drove off.

Theo stood in front of Evelyn's house for a few minutes, reminiscing on old memories, like how he had often dropped her off at her house with his buggy and talked to her until her mother started calling her name. Or, how he'd climbed the tree behind their house so he could place a note on her windowpane.

When his injured leg began to throb, he slowly made his way to the front door and knocked. The scent of baking wafted to his nostrils, reminding him of how he'd missed Evelyn's pastries, but the tension that knotted in his stomach made him unable to dwell on the pleasant aroma.

What if she wasn't home? What if she didn't live here anymore?

"Breathe, Theo," he told himself. "Whatever happens, know that you at least tried."

The door opened, and Beverly Yoder stared at him with wide eyes.

"Theo? What are you doing here?" she said, her voice filled with surprise, then anger.

"Hello, Mrs. Yoder," he said, hoping she wouldn't slam the door in his face. The Amish weren't prone to slamming doors, but if Evelyn's mother decided to, he deserved it.

Her eyes went from his face to the crutch and his legs. The angry look on her face morphed into resignation. With a clenched jaw and furrowed brows, she said in a barely civil voice, "Come in."

Theo walked into the house and sat down. He placed the crutch by the side of the chair, his eyes watching her as she went to the kitchen. There were now two bookshelves in the living room as opposed to only one when he'd left. The second bookshelf wasn't full yet. He could bet that most of the books were Evelyn's, and the rest were for her father.

Beverly placed a plate of cookies in front of him.

"Thank you. Is Evelyn home? I came to see her," he said.

Beverly sat on the sofa opposite and watched him in silence.

"Is she... Is she married?" he asked tentatively.

Beverly only narrowed her eyes. Clearly, he wouldn't get any answers from her. He reached forward, taking a cookie from the plate. The moment Theo bit into it, the flavor burst in his mouth, and he hummed in satisfaction. He'd frequently made that sound when he had eaten Evelyn's pastries because they were delicious, and Beverly usually smiled in response.

But now, Beverly stared at him with a deepening frown. He lowered his eyes.

"I know me coming back here is a shock, but I just want to know how Evelyn is. I'd really love to see her," he said in a low voice.

She only stared at him. The cookies didn't seem so delicious anymore. When the silence became unbearable, Beverly stood up and walked out of the living room toward the kitchen.

"You should talk to her about this. It's not my place to answer. Evelyn will soon be back from work," she said curtly on her way out.

He sat and waited for Evelyn. So, was she married? Was that why her mother wouldn't answer? But if she was, why would she be coming here after work? About twenty minutes later, which seemed like twenty hours, he heard her voice before the front door opened.

Evelyn's sweet voice filled the room. "*Maem*, I bought another book from the store. I know you said I shouldn't spend all my money buying books, but the story was so good. I want to read it again. I..."

She abruptly paused by the front door, speechless, as her eyes locked on Theo's.

The sunlight illuminated her from behind, silhouetting her delicate shape. She was more beautiful than the last time he'd seen her, and the light in her eyes had never dimmed, unlike his.

Theo stood up, balancing his weight on his good leg. As a matter of pride, he didn't pick up his crutch. He wanted her to see how strong and muscular he'd grown in the Army. Let his Evelyn see him without the crutch before associating weakness with him.

"Th...Theo," she stammered.

"Evelyn," he said, putting in all the emotion and love he'd developed for her in that one word.

Chapter Seventeen

Evelyn stared at the love of her life with growing alarm. She stood, unable to move, as if she'd seen a ghost. She felt the walls closing in, the air too heavy to breathe. Theo had said he wasn't coming back. He'd moved to a new base without giving her a forwarding address and had stopped sending her letters. But he was standing in her living room.

Wow. Finally, she blinked, and he looked even more handsome and muscular. Something in his eyes, a mysterious darkness, drew her to him, and she longed to hold him close and ask him to tell her everything that had happened to him.

When she heard her mother washing dishes in the kitchen, she snapped out of her trance, then closed the front door. Moving past Theo without sparing him another glance so she wouldn't lose her courage, she placed the book on the shelf. Her hand froze on the book. She stared at it solemnly, knowing she needed to tell him the news about her and Steven. She opened her mouth to make the statement she was sure would break both their hearts.

"Eve," he said. His footsteps moving closer seemed to beat in rhythm with her heart. "How are you? What has happened while I was away? Are you...married?"

"You need to leave." Her voice was shrill, panicked. She should tell him she was engaged to his brother, and the wedding was four months away, but she was no longer in control of her mental faculties or her mouth. Instead, she said, "You can't be here."

"Eve, please. Let me explain."

She waited for him to give some paltry excuse for his deception.

"I'm sorry for telling you I wouldn't be coming back," he said.

A flash of anger went through her. She turned toward him but stopped short of facing him fully.

"While you're at it, you can apologize for your actions from the beginning. You left the Amish, then left me after indicating interest in a romantic relationship. Your only warning before joining the military was a note on my window. When I received your letter, I forgave you so easily and replied. You left me again and told me you wouldn't be coming back. I have been waiting for you for six years. Six years!" she cried, quickly wiping tears from her burning eyes as shock, anger, and love for him welled up within her. Why was she feeling these things? She shouldn't be. It was so unfair to Steven—it wasn't right. "Now, you're here. You'll probably leave again, won't you?"

He grunted, moved back to the sofa, and sat down. His hands went through his hair which was cut short, especially on the sides, in a military haircut. His eyes closed briefly, a grimace on his face.

"I messed up. I'm so sorry."

From her peripheral vision, she assessed him. He'd definitely grown more muscular, his shoulders and torso filling out his shirt. His short hair made his face look more mature. Before she could display caution, she found herself gazing at him and appreciating what she saw.

"Is that all you're going to say?" she replied.

"When I was eighteen, I had only two goals—to join the Army and to get married to you. I never saw them as two opposing things. I thought I'd be able to fuse them together by asking you to join me and leave. But that day, when I asked you how you felt about leaving the community and saw the revulsion on your face, I knew it wouldn't be fair to you or your parents to convince you to go with me. Although it was excruciating, I refrained from courting you and left."

"Then why didn't you tell me you were going for basic training before leaving?"

He sighed. "You would have pleaded with me to stay, and I'd have listened."

She harrumphed and crossed her arms over her chest.

"I couldn't bear to see the judgment on your face on telling you I was planning to do the exact thing you condemned. I didn't want to see the hurt in your eyes. I was looking out for you by not telling you."

Evelyn lowered her voice so her mother wouldn't hear, who was still washing dishes. "Oh please, if your intentions were so noble, why did you start corresponding with me? The worst part was you didn't send any letters to your family."

He was silent for a while, then he spoke. "I missed you so much, I had to communicate. I wanted to read your sweet words and form a stronger bond with you. I hoped that someday we'd get married despite the circumstances and distance between us."

"Then why did you stop sending the letters? Why did you say you were not coming back to the Amish only to mysteriously appear here today?"

"I was wrong, Eve. I thought joining the Army and becoming a national hero would make me feel fulfilled." He chuckled bitterly. "Instead, I became a shell filled with gruesome memories of the lives I took. There was no happiness there for me, no family. Despite being on the frontlines like I always wanted, I yearned to be with you every day."

She rubbed her temples and shook her head. It was time to tell him that his coming back to Unity was for naught. She was engaged to Steven and was planning to marry him, even though seeing Theo had made her heart beat faster than all the times she'd been with his brother.

Her longing for Theo was increasing by the second. She wanted to bask in his warm embrace and tell him how she'd dreamt of marrying him. She wanted to talk about all those years when she'd missed his presence. But that would neither strengthen her cause nor help her predicament.

It didn't matter if she still loved Theo and was suppressing the urge to run into his arms. She would soon be his brother's wife. She'd made a promise to give her whole heart to Steven. Now that she'd almost succeeded, Theo decided to saunter back into her life. Unfortunately, his presence didn't change past events. The Amish community, their parents, the elders, and the bishop knew about her and Steven's courtship. The wedding date was already set. It was time to inform Theo about it.

Theo stood up, and she snapped her head away, unable to look at him while delivering the news. He slowly moved towards her.

"Theo, I..."

He gingerly knelt before her where she stood, taking her hands in his. At his touch, sparks of electricity shot through her entire body, sending butterflies dancing in her stomach—so far beyond anything she'd ever felt for Steven.

Oh yes, she still loved Theo. She loved him with everything in her.

"Evelyn, will you marry me?" he asked, peering into her eyes.

Her world shattered. A strangled sound came out of her mouth.

"I know my proposal is abrupt. But we've been apart for so long, and I don't want to miss another opportunity to court you. I want to live with you and grow old with you, Eve, and not spend another day without you."

"It's too late," she whispered.

"Why?" he asked, moving closer. "Are you married? Please, tell me. Just tell me. The suspense is literally killing me."

"We can't get married. I can't marry you, Theo."

She stared at her feet, realizing that he'd come overwhelmingly close. His woody and spicy scent filled the atmosphere, intoxicating her. He stood up laboriously and leaned on the bookshelf, cocking his head in confusion. There was something different about him. Besides the fact that the Theo she knew didn't lean on things—shelves, walls, doors, or any furniture—he looked less confident.

"Have you fallen in love with someone else?" he whispered. "If you're married, why would you come home after work?"

She couldn't lie to him. She kept staring at her feet.

His voice became bolder. "Look me in the eye and tell me you don't love me. I know you do. Or is there something else you need to tell me?"

Evelyn felt tears prick her eyelids. Where had Theo been when she'd needed him? Now, he wanted to use love as an excuse to win her back. What of commitment, loyalty, taking care of her, proving that he'd never abandon her?

"I'm engaged. The wedding is this November," she choked out. "That's why we can't get married."

She could see different emotions rushing through his face. First bewilderment, then regrets and a host of other emotions, before it settled into steely determination.

"It's just an engagement. We can find a way to appeal to your fiancé. Then we'll get married."

Her head shook vigorously from side to side. "It's not that simple. I won't do that. Besides, we have been apart for six years. We are both different people now." She knew that didn't matter, that she still loved him anyway, even after all their time apart. Her heart broke a little more.

"Do you love him?" When she didn't reply, he continued, "If you don't love him, why did you get engaged to him? Eve, I'll talk to him. I'll do anything to make sure he understands that you and I are meant to be together."

"You don't understand. It won't work. I can't get married to you." She shook her head, trying not to melt into a fit of sobs.

He reached out to hold her arms. She stepped back, knowing that she would crumble into his embrace the moment he touched her.

"Eve, who is he?" he asked hoarsely.

The tears fell down her cheeks then. "I'm getting married to Steven, your brother."

Theo froze, a perfect picture of alarm. He stood still for a while, then moved back to the sofa. She watched in horror as he hopped to the side and picked up a crutch. He slowly made his way to the front door and held the doorknob. His shoulders deflated.

"I need a buggy to get home. I'd walk, but I..." his voice trailed off as he looked down at his crutch. "Can I use yours? I'll bring it back tomorrow."

"Yes."

He walked out of the house with an uneven gait.

Evelyn had thought she'd given her heart to Steven and deleted every memory of his brother. But her love for Theo had not dissipated, not one bit. On the contrary, she was aware of him in a way she'd never been aware of any other man. The memory of their conversation played over and over again in her head; his emotions, his voice that soothed her, his chiseled jaw and caring eyes, his fragrance that she could still smell, the way he called her name.

Evelyn realized the truth then. She loved Theo, and no matter how hard she tried not to, she would always love him. Whatever feelings she had for Steven were insignificant in comparison. It was a slight feeling of comfort and security.

At that moment, Evelyn didn't know what was worse—the fact that Theo's leg was injured and he needed a crutch or the fact that she had to marry his brother even though her heart still beat for him.

She picked the book back up from the shelf and headed to the stairs. If she read the story tonight, she wouldn't have to think of Theo, Steven, or her warring emotions. Her mother rushed out of the kitchen to meet her. Evelyn hugged her, shuddering. She stayed there for a long while, enjoying the gentle pat of her mother's hand on her back until she no longer felt like she was breaking apart.

Chapter Eighteen

Theo hobbled out of the house and towards the buggy, his injured leg throbbing. He had made several huge mistakes and didn't know which to correct first.

He drove the buggy to where his luggage lay on the ground, got down, and managed to put the box in while memories of Evelyn flooded his mind. Seeing her had made him realize how much he'd hurt her. Her eyes had been filled with anger and accusation.

He wondered if his family felt the same way. Would they forgive him for leaving the Amish and joining the Army? Would they welcome him back despite his not writing any letters home? Theo knew he had to face Ivan, Linda, and Steven and ask for forgiveness. He climbed into the buggy and drove towards his childhood home, his heart heavy with sadness and regret.

He drove the buggy without having to think about it. After all this time, he still remembered how. As he approached the house, he saw his father and mother in front of the farmhouse. When his head poked out from the buggy, they stared at him for a few seconds, then wide smiles enveloped their faces.

A wave of relief washed over Theo. His parents were happy to see him!

Except for the greenhouse at the far end of the field, the farm was just as he remembered it—the sheep, horses, and cows in the pasture, the barn off to the side, and the farmhouse in the center. The smell of the grass and manure was soothing to him. The neighing, mooing, and bleating of the animals grazing peacefully was a balm to his soul. He forgot all about his troubles and enjoyed being home for a moment. He sat in the buggy, soaking in the atmosphere as a cool breeze tickled the hairs on his skin.

Finally, Theo grasped his crutch and got down from the buggy. His parents hurried toward him, Linda's skirt flying behind her.

"Theo!" his mother cried, tears already coursing down her face.

"We are so glad you're home, son," his father choked out, throwing his arms around his son. Theo embraced his father and mother warmly. Tears ran down Linda's cheeks while Ivan's eyes were moist with tears.

"Theo, you were gone for so long." Linda clutched his arms, finally pulling away to look at him.

"My son," Ivan said, his voice filled with emotion, and hugged him again. "All that matters is you're home now."

"*Daed, Maem*, I'm sorry for everything," Theo said contritely. "I was young and headstrong, and I thought having my way was the best possible choice. I've been away for so many years without communicating with you. Can you ever forgive me?"

"Of course, we can. All is forgiven. You're our son, and we love you no matter what," his father said. He patted Theo on the back and then helped him with his luggage.

"Of course, we forgive you, dear. Now, come inside and sit down!" his mother cried, staring at him admiringly. "Let's get you settled in. Let me make you something to eat."

Theo's heart swelled with happiness at his family's forgiveness. It dawned on him that he had not seen his brother.

"Where's Steven?" he asked.

"He's out on farm business. He should be back soon," Linda replied.

Theo and his parents went into the living room. He sat on the sofa; it was as sturdy as the last time he'd sat on it. Ivan was still smiling and looking at him like he was a gift from heaven. Linda's face, however, was pinched into a frown.

"Theo, tell us what happened," she said gently, gesturing to his leg. "How did you get hurt?"

Theo shifted uncomfortably. He didn't want to talk about the infamous battle or his injuries. It was hard enough dealing with the nightmares and flashbacks. Instinctively, he hid the crutch behind the sofa so his parents wouldn't focus on it. But he knew his mother deserved an explanation.

"I was shot in the stomach and leg when I was saving fellow soldiers on the battlefield. I was unconscious in the hospital for several months due to head trauma I sustained from the fall." He paused, noticing that Linda was getting increasingly distressed, and rushed on. "I underwent physical therapy when I became well enough to be discharged. I've been using a crutch since then."

"And what about mentally?" Ivan asked. "I hope you're not having any problems in that area."

Theo looked away. He didn't want to taint his family by describing his nightmares. "I've been having constant nightmares."

His parents' eyes widened then their faces took on pitiful looks.

"They're just bad dreams," he continued quickly. "I don't want to talk about them. I also lost my best friend."

Linda nodded understandingly, rushing to his side. "We are so sorry, Theo. It must have been awful for you. We're glad you're safe and back home," she said, touching his hand.

He looked down at his mother's hand on his and felt a surge of love.

"It was, *Maem*," he replied quietly. "But I'm alive, and that's what matters."

Ivan placed a hand on his shoulder. "We are very sorry to hear about your friend, Theo, but we're glad you're home."

Theo nodded, his throat constricting with emotion. He was grateful to be alive and to be home with his family. They'd forgiven him without hesitation and welcomed him back with open arms. It was more than he could have ever asked for. He looked at his parents, really looked at them, and saw the wisdom in their eyes and realized just how much they seemed to age in the six years he was gone. He realized he'd been foolish to deceive them and leave the Amish community. He belonged here with his family.

"I want to be baptized into the church. I want to be part of the community again."

"Oh!" Linda cried gleefully, clapping her hands together. "What wonderful news!"

"We will go to Bishop Byler tomorrow and arrange it," Ivan said, nodding. "It is indeed the best news we could hope for. All these years, we prayed for you to come home safely, and God has answered our prayers." Ivan looked heavenward. "Thank you, Lord. This is a cause for celebration!"

Theo couldn't help but smile. He was finally home where he belonged.

But how could he live here if he saw the woman of his dreams marry his brother?

After downing a delicious meal made by his mother, Theo inspected the farm. He marveled at the massive greenhouse, larger gardens, and all the new changes. The place had prospered after he left. The workers were industrious and dexterous, too. His father must have taught them well.

Theo felt a pang of jealousy, followed by regret. If he'd stayed, he could have been part of this. Then the Amish community would have seen him as honorable. But it was too late for that now.

The sound of a buggy driving into the farm made him look up. Steven had returned, and the buggy came to a stop. He jumped down, glaring at Theo. Steven's face was set in a deep frown, and his eyes were cold and disapproving. It was clear that he didn't approve of his brother's presence on the farm.

"Evelyn said you were back," Steven said coldly. "I thought I should come see for myself."

Theo still couldn't wrap his mind around Steven being Evelyn's fiancé. He'd tried to push the knowledge of their engagement into the deep recesses of his mind, where he wouldn't ever be able to dig it out, but he was still surprised and disappointed about the news.

Did Evelyn tell Steven about the discussion they'd had? His brother would have picked up on her lingering love for Theo if she did. That must be the cause of his anger. Theo decided to be conciliatory. He'd ask for his brother's forgiveness first, then sort the rest out later. He took a step forward, but Steven held up his hand.

"Don't come any closer," he warned. "You're not welcome here."

Theo was taken aback by his brother's hostility. He'd expected some tension between them but not this level of animosity. He leaned on the wall of the greenhouse and breathed in deeply to stay calm.

"I'm not here to cause any trouble. I was admiring the farm and seeing how *Daed* has been taking care of it. It's much more advanced since I left."

"*Daed* and *Maem* have been sick so much that I am the one who has been taking care of the farm."

"I'm sorry," Theo said, a pang of guilt slamming him in the chest.

"Of course, you wouldn't know. Sometimes they were sick for weeks at a time."

Evelyn had told him that, but he just stared at the ground.

"They probably didn't want you to feel bad about it. I introduced the idea of getting a greenhouse, and we built it without your help," Steven spat out. He opened his mouth to say a few choice words, then closed it and stomped into the barn.

Theo looked around the farm. The workers, who had been listening to the conversation, averted their eyes and left for the day.

Steven had done a good job. He clearly had taken charge of the farm after Theo left, but that didn't mean he should have gotten engaged to Eve.

Theo loved Evelyn deeply. They'd formed a strong bond while writing letters to each other all those years, even though they had stopped a while ago. He wanted to marry her, and he knew that she still loved him. He'd seen it in her eyes while they talked by the bookshelf.

There was no way he would let Steven marry her. Evelyn was the love of his life. Steven could find someone else.

Theo would fight for Evelyn. He'd make her realize that they belonged together. Theo knew it wouldn't be easy to get her to end the engagement, but he was determined to win his Evelyn back. He knew without a doubt that he was the one Evelyn loved and that she was only staying engaged to Steven because she'd made a commitment. Theo had to make her realize that she belonged with him before it was too late, and they would both regret it.

He just hoped she would be willing to give him a second chance.

Once Theo had a plan of action, he started implementing it. He'd learned in the Army to act fast on the battlefield. Right now, he was battling with Steven for Evelyn's heart, and he intended to win.

He walked into the barn and sat on a stool. Steven ignored him.

"I know you and Evelyn are engaged."

Steven huffed. "What do you care?"

"I care about Eve. I love her."

"You have no right to say that. You abandoned her when she needed you the most. Meanwhile, I've been here for her." Steven glanced at him nervously. For the first time, Theo saw the younger brother he knew.

Hot jealousy burned through Theo at the thought of Steven and Evelyn being engaged. "Evelyn and I have been exchanging letters for years."

The brush nearly fell from Steven's hand. "You're lying."

Theo could see the realization dawn on Steven's face and surmised that his brother didn't know about the letters. He knew he had hit a nerve. He gave Steven a slight smile and stood up.

"You can ask her yourself." He took a step closer and lowered his voice. "She never told you about it because she cherishes my letters so much, and I asked her not to tell anyone. She only stopped writing when I told her I would never come back home even after I was out of the military."

"It can't be true," Steven said, stepping back. But his voice wavered, and his face took on a pained expression. "Evelyn would have told me."

"I know I still have a chance with her. She loves me, not you."

As he said that, a pang of guilt hit his chest. He'd not come back to Unity to fight with Steven. He'd come back to ask for his forgiveness and rebuild their relationship. But, here he was, acting like his brother was his enemy.

Yet he knew that he had to weaken Steven's defenses. It was the only way to have a chance with Evelyn.

A shadow fell across the barn door. Theo turned and saw their father standing by the door, a huge grin on his face.

"Well, Theo, your return calls for a celebration," he said, his voice booming in the barn. He spread his arms out in excitement. "I've always hoped this day would come. It's so good to have you back home."

Ivan enveloped Theo in another bear hug. A deep scowl appeared on Steven's face. Ivan stepped back and held Theo at arm's length.

"Your *maem* has started planning for the event already."

"Thank you, *Daed*," he mumbled, his guilt for how he'd just treated Steven increasing.

His father and mother hadn't judged him because they were older and more mature. Theo couldn't say the same for himself. Just a little condemnation and rivalry from his younger brother, and he'd acted harshly. Theo excused himself from the barn and went into the farmhouse.

Chapter Nineteen

Steven watched Theo's retreating back until he couldn't see him anymore. He turned and started cleaning the barn, fear and anger thrumming through him. He angrily flung the muck out of the stall, not caring where it landed.

His mind was consumed with thoughts of Theo and the pain he'd caused by leaving the Amish community over six years ago. Then, his brother had only been cocky, selfish, and deceptive. Now, he'd added meanness to his list of attributes.

When Evelyn had told Steven about Theo's arrival, she'd had a guarded expression. She'd spoken with a voice full of concern, asking him to consider his brother's predicament.

Steven had scoffed and crossed his arms over his chest. "He left us all those years ago and never looked back."

Evelyn had hesitated for a moment, then sighed. "He's changed. He seems different now—more mature, maybe even a little humble."

"Yeah right. I'm sure that's just an act to win *Daed's* favor."

Evelyn frowned. "Don't be so quick to judge him before giving him a chance, Steven. He's your brother."

He hadn't said his next hurt-filled words out loud, but he'd said them in his mind: *He's not my brother anymore. I don't want anything to do with him.*

Presently, he tried to focus on his cleaning task. It didn't matter that Theo had been gone for so long. It didn't even matter that he was supposed to be repentant. All that mattered was that he'd come back and was trying to take what was rightfully Steven's.

Evelyn.

His heart clenched painfully in his chest as he thought of her. She was the one person who connected fully with him. Their heart had become one. And now, his brother was trying to take her away from him forcefully.

He recalled Theo's cynical voice dripping with intimidation as he spoke about sending letters to Evelyn. Did they truly exchange letters? Did they have a long-distance relationship he was unaware of?

Steven shook his head. No. Evelyn would have told him about it. She'd never lie to him.

On the other hand, Theo had lied six years ago when he'd pretended to want a farm, causing his father to take out a loan that the family had to repay, and then he'd callously left.

Steven decided to trust Evelyn's love. She'd told him about her feelings for Theo and him. She would have told him about the letters if there were any or if they were important enough. If she'd written to Theo in the past, then she'd decided to forget it and focus on Steven. Evelyn would still want to be with him despite his brother's return. He'd cultivated a relationship with her, unlike Theo, who hadn't been around and thought he could barge into their lives. Evelyn loved Steven, and that was that.

Ivan cleared his throat.

"*Daed,*" Steven said, unable to come up with any other word.

He couldn't believe that his father had actually welcomed Theo back into the family without a second thought. Where was the justice in that? How could Theo still manage to gain favor when he'd left the community for a life outside of God's law, a life that included violence and killing? It wasn't fair, and it made Steven burn with anger.

Ivan was still at the door, giving him a contemplative gaze.

"Steven, come here," he said, beckoning him over.

Reluctantly, Steven walked toward his father.

"Why did you announce a celebration, *Daed*? Theo doesn't deserve it," he said, his voice tight.

"Your brother has been gone for over six years. He's finally come back, and he will be baptized into the church. I want to celebrate that."

"Why are you celebrating Theo after he abandoned us? He put us in debt and made us work so hard. How can you even think about celebrating him after everything he's done?"

"I'm not celebrating him because of what he did. He was lost to the Amish community, but now he's found. He left us, but now he's back. I've regained a son," Ivan said with a wistful smile.

Steven's heart constricted. His father had never talked about him in that manner. "But you never celebrated me despite all the time and effort I put into the farm."

"Steven," Ivan said, placing a hand on his shoulder. His father's touch had a way of calming him; it was the ice to his flaming hot anger. "We appreciate everything you've done. You know that. Again, I'm celebrating his return, not what he's done. Don't compare yourself to your brother; you're different. Give him a chance. Don't judge him before getting to know what he went through in the Army."

Ivan's words penetrated his heart, making Steven contrite. Theo had an injured leg, and Steven hadn't bothered to ask about it. But then, his brother had always manipulated people for his own gain. Could it be that he'd only come back to the Amish because he'd sustained an injury that made him unfit to serve in the Army? Steven didn't want his family to be at the receiving end of Theo's scheming. Shaking his head, he opened his mouth to explain to his father.

"Listen to me, son," Ivan cut in. "I understand that you're angry with your brother and the way he treated us years ago. But I believe in giving people second chances, especially when they've come back repentant. Remember all the bishop taught you about overcoming anger."

Steven nodded. He'd promised himself he wouldn't let negative emotions get the best of him.

He made up his mind not to let Theo get under his skin. He wouldn't give his brother the satisfaction of seeing him angry, jealous, or uncertain again. Instead, Steven would show him what it meant to live a good and righteous life, which honored God above all things.

And then, somehow, he would find a way to make sure that Theo knew how hurtful his actions had been towards their family and his Amish faith. Steven would prove that he was the better choice, the man who acted based on God's love, the one who had made the farm prosper, and the appropriate husband for Evelyn. That, Steven was sure of. And he would prove it to everyone, including Theo.

Chapter Twenty

As the days passed, Evelyn couldn't help but return to the habit of comparing Steven and Theo. It was inevitable, really. They were both similar in many ways, yet so different in others. Theo and Steven looked alike. Yet, Theo was taller and had broader shoulders, while Steven was a bit shorter and thinner.

While both were equally handsome, Evelyn couldn't help but feel drawn to Theo in a way she couldn't explain. Theo was the wild one who always seemed to dash off into his adventures. There was a certain charm about him that was impossible to resist. She had always been drawn to him.

Now, he was back home on the farm, injured, and dependent on crutches. Evelyn's heart went out to him, even as her mind filled with questions. What had happened to him out there on the battlefield? How had he gotten hurt? He must have been quite brave and strong.

She hadn't shared these thoughts with Steven, of course. She couldn't risk betraying her love for Theo by letting Steven know how she felt about his estranged brother. It was enough that she had to deal with the guilt of being engaged to Steven while still harboring feelings for Theo.

Evelyn tried her best to put Theo out of her mind, knowing that she had made a commitment to Steven and shouldn't turn back now. But it got harder not to think about him whenever she went to the farm, especially as she watched him struggle with his injury every day. Even now, when she should have been focused on preparing for her wedding, her mind wandered back to him whenever it got the chance. She kept wondering how he was doing and what kind of person he'd become after his gruesome experience on the frontlines.

She found herself frequently sighing and humming in the bookstore, at the farmer's market, while baking at home, and when she was talking to her parents. Thoughts of Theo had captured her mind. She couldn't let go of her feelings for him. He was too special to her, and part of her had always known it would be this way.

Some members of the Amish community had started calling Theo a prodigal son. In a sense, Evelyn felt like a prodigal herself. Just as Theo had returned to his family after going so long without them, so had she come back into contact with the person who had been in her heart all along.

To her utmost despair, her love for him grew even stronger despite minimal contact. She couldn't tell her mother about her dilemma since she hadn't confided in her when she'd been corresponding with Theo.

She turned to her friends instead. Livia met at her house one evening along with their friend, Laura. Evelyn had picked Laura up from the farmer's market while Livia had arrived sometime before the two of them. While they were drinking milk and eating cake that tasted bland to Evelyn because her mind was clouded with worry, Laura spoke up, eyes twinkling.

"Eve, I'm sure you didn't call us here to have a cake party. I can already guess what's troubling you. Does it by any chance have to do with the Glicks?"

Evelyn sighed. "Yes. Theo is back."

"What does that have to do with anything?" Livia asked.

"I don't like admitting this, but I'm in love with Theo," she answered simply, not trusting herself to say more.

"What? But you're engaged to his brother! You promised to love Steven," Livia protested.

"I know, I know," Evelyn said, her voice filled with despair. "I can't help it. I've tried to give my heart to Steven, but it's so difficult now that Theo is back. I thought I could let go of Theo and give my heart to Steven, but I'm not sure anymore."

Livia looked away, shaking her head in disappointment.

"Have you talked to Theo or Steven?" Laura asked, placing a warm, comforting arm around her shoulder.

"No, of course not. I promised to forget about Theo and move on with my life." She looked from Laura to Livia, remembering when she'd made that promise to Livia. "I even asked Steven for a long courtship so I could become fully committed to him, but it's hard when I keep thinking about Theo. I've always loved Theo."

"You made a commitment to Steven, Evelyn. You can't just turn back on that now. He would be hurt and feel betrayed," Livia said.

She hung her head in sorrow. "But I don't know what to do. I'm torn between two men—one who has always been good to me and one who is like a dream come true. If I'm in love with Theo, should I call off my wedding before it's too late?"

Laura rubbed her shoulder. "What do you really want? Who makes your heart beat faster?"

Evelyn didn't have to think about it before answering. "It's Theo," she admitted quietly. "He's always been the one for me, even though he left years ago without saying goodbye. Now he's back, and I can't stop thinking about him."

"So, what are you going to do?" Laura asked as Livia pushed the cake around on her plate silently.

Evelyn shook her head, at a loss for words. She was torn between two men; one she had always loved and one she was slowly starting to care for. The way she felt about Steven was nothing like what she felt for Theo—she loved him with her whole heart, recklessly and desperately. One thing was for sure; she had to figure out a way to sort out her feelings before she could move on with her life.

Anxiety pulsed through Evelyn's body as she tried to decide what to do about her relationship with Steven and her feelings for Theo. "Theo asked me to marry him. What if I gently tell Steven that we can no longer get married and pursue my feelings for Theo?"

"You can't just break Steven's heart like that," Livia said, her voice laced with anger. "He's been through a lot, and he doesn't deserve to be hurt by you."

"But I can't help how I feel. Theo is the one I love, and I can't deny that. It wouldn't be fair to Steven if I took that into our marriage."

"You chose to love Steven and commit to him," Livia replied firmly. "You must forget about Theo."

"I can't! I don't know why I ever thought I could. Now that he's here, it's impossible. I'd be living a lie if I married

Steven!" Evelyn cried out, her fists slamming the table, her mind racing.

Her friends became silent.

"Steven has always been there for his family, even when Theo deserted them. He took care of his sick parents and managed the farm by himself. He has been loyal to his family and to you, unlike Theo. You should think of that before you run into Theo's arms." Livia stood up abruptly. Her voice trembled as she continued, "I can't believe you would consider breaking Steven's heart like that. He's been through so much, and he doesn't deserve to be hurt by you. You should stick to your commitment to him. Besides, Theo is flighty. What if he leaves again? Then what? You'll end up alone."

She turned and walked out of the house, leaving Evelyn with her thoughts. Laura stayed with her, comforting her.

"I've never seen Livia like that before," Evelyn choked out, wiping a tear from her eye that had formed during her friend's blunt words.

"She just wants what's best for you." Laura patted Evelyn's back.

Evelyn had a difficult choice to make. She sat, lost in thought as she wrestled with her dilemma. She could continue her relationship with Steven and give up on her feelings for Theo, or she could break it off with Steven in pursuit of the man she truly loved.

But what if Livia was right? What if Theo left again? Then what? She would have lost both of her chances at love.

Whichever path she chose, there would be inevitable pain and heartbreak for one of the brothers. She just hoped that she'd make the right decision in the end.

"What am I going to do?" she whispered to herself.

"Eve, I know how you feel about Theo. You've loved him for years and always wanted to be with him. But then he left, and I thought you had overcome those feelings. When you and Steven started dating, and I saw the way you looked at him, I was elated. Finally, you were going to get married to someone who loved you and could unequivocally reciprocate your feelings. But now," Laura said. "I'm not so sure. Eve, I think the first step to solving this problem is for you to think back to when you accepted Steven's proposal. What did you see in him? What made you think he would make a good husband? Why did you decide to get married to him?"

Evelyn's mind wandered back to when she'd agreed to court Steven.

"I guess I saw in him the same qualities that Theo has always possessed. He was confident and bold. He was also filled with assurance. In some ways, he reminds me of Theo. Besides that, he's kind and loyal. He cares deeply for his family. He's also a hard worker, and he's always been there for me."

"And do you still see those qualities in him? Or have your feelings for Theo made you blind to them?"

Evelyn was quiet for a moment as she considered Laura's question.

"I still see those qualities in him," Evelyn said finally. "But I'm not sure if I fell in love with him because I saw those qualities or if I was seeing Theo in him. Maybe that made me accept his proposal. And to be honest, I'm not sure which one is more important to me. I care for both of them deeply, and I don't want to hurt either one of them."

"So, what are you going to do?"

She sighed again. "I need some time to think about it."

"I think that's a good idea," Laura said softly. "Just don't let too much time pass. You need to make a decision soon, or you might end up hurting both men."

Evelyn nodded slowly.

When Steven visited Evelyn, his face was sullen like it had been when Theo joined the Army. As he climbed down from the buggy, Evelyn walked towards him tentatively, no longer sure of her feelings.

"Evelyn," he said gruffly as he came to a stop in front of her. "I need to talk to you."

"What is it?" she asked, her heart beating erratically in her chest.

Steven held her hand and took her to a bed of flowers her mother had planted. Evelyn glanced at their interlocked hands. Steven's touch felt ordinary, a bit warm like the comforting touch of a friend. It wasn't sizzling hot like she instinctively knew Theo's hand would feel. Evelyn removed her hand and made a show of adjusting her *kapp*.

"I didn't want to ask you this because I trust you, but it's been bothering me a lot." Steven paused as a flash of hurt crossed his eyes. "I know about the letters. I know you've been writing to Theo for years."

Evelyn took a step back, feeling like she'd been punched in the stomach. "How did you find out?"

"Theo gloated about it. He thought I should know," he said bitterly. "At first, I didn't believe him. But something in his voice made me feel he was telling the truth."

"And what do you think?" she asked in a shaky voice.

"I wanted to ask you about it. What would you call the letter exchange between you and Theo?"

"I never gave it a label," she said in a small voice. "We were just sending letters to each other. He sent me a letter shortly after going to boot camp, and I replied."

Steven's eyes widened, and she shrank back.

"I think you've been carrying on a long-distance relationship with my brother, even though you never gave it a name."

"It's not like that." She shook her head, knowing she was lying. Every time she saw one of those letters arrive, her heart had soared. She'd looked forward to writing to him and hearing from him.

Of course, it had been a long-distance relationship.

"Did it occur to you to tell us about his letters or ask if we were exchanging letters with him? When *Daed* and *Maem* were ill, I tried to contact Theo. I sent letters to an address Sergeant Mills gave me." His face took on a faraway look as if recalling a painful past. "The address was wrong. If I'd known someone so close to me always knew Theo's whereabouts…" His voice trailed off.

"I'm sorry, Steven. I should have told you, but he asked me not to tell anyone." Guilt and shame gnawed at her heart, and she wrapped her arms around herself. "At that point, it was too difficult for me to tell you I'd been writing to him for so long, but I should have."

"Of course, he asked you not to give us his address. I'm not surprised. Still, even when you saw how sick my parents were, you should have given it to me so I could let him know. Maybe he would have come home then."

Evelyn sighed. "You're right, Steven. I'm so sorry."

"What I really want to know is the extent of your relationship with my brother in those letters," Steven asked, peering at her intently.

"We were just friends," she replied, too afraid to tell him the truth.

"The type of friend that asked you to marry him before he left for the military? Didn't he tell you he loved you in those letters?"

Evelyn was speechless. Stephen huffed when she didn't speak.

"Friends don't exchange intimate letters for years. There was something more between you two. I want you to admit it."

Evelyn had never thought about defining what she and Theo had when they'd written to each other. But...yes, it was a long-distance relationship. And now the secret was out. Now, Steven knew about her correspondence with his brother.

Yet, she couldn't admit it to his face. Steven knew how to brood. If she gave the correspondence between her and Theo a romantic name, her fiancé would keep thinking about it for days. Years even. The thoughts would churn in his mind until he exploded.

She had to tell him the truth.

"I'm sorry," she said, her voice barely above a whisper. "I never meant to hurt you."

Steven turned away from her, his shoulders hunched. Evelyn reached out to touch his arm, but he shrugged her off.

"Please, Steven. Don't be angry with me," she pleaded.

"Why didn't you tell me?" he said, his voice raw with emotion.

"I didn't tell you because Theo said he wasn't coming back, and I burned the letters," Evelyn defended herself.

"You should have told me. I had a right to know."

"Why? So, you could be angry with me and accuse me? How would that have helped us?"

"I'm not angry with you, Eve. I'm just hurt that you didn't trust me enough to tell me the truth. Had Theo not stopped writing to you, would you have accepted my proposal?"

Evelyn was silent. There was no way she could answer that question honestly. She had loved Theo most of her life, and there were so many moments when she'd wished he would return.

"I have a right to know about your correspondence with my brother," he said sternly. "You had no reason to keep it a secret from me. If you had told me the truth, we would have dealt with it together."

Evelyn hung her head in shame. Steven turned and walked away without another word, leaving her alone in a cloud of regret.

She stood on the porch, watching as he drove away in his buggy, drifting away from her.

She remembered how she, Theo, and Steven played on the farm when they were children. It had been a glorious time filled with laughter and rolling around in the coarse hay. She recalled fondly when they'd poured flour all over the kitchen floor. While Theo's mother was out, Evelyn had boasted that she could bake and proceeded to demonstrate to the two boys. The flour bag had slipped and fallen. Some of it fell out. Theo had proposed the ingenious idea that the smooth flour could be pretend snow inside the house. The three children had gone on to rub it all over their faces and arms, pouring the rest of the flour on the floor in the process.

Evelyn smiled at the memory, but then the smile faded. She cared for Theo and Steven deeply, but things between the three of them were turning awry. She felt bad about the discussion she'd had with Steven and didn't want to be the cause of problems between the two brothers.

Evelyn walked back to her house slowly, her heart heavy with sadness.

I have to fix this somehow, she thought desperately.

But she didn't know how or where to start.

Chapter Twenty-one

Theo sat at the dining table, his hands clasped loosely in front of him. His father and mother were at the table, their faces tense with anticipation as they waited for Steven to join them. The tension was palpable; it almost suffocated Theo in its intensity.

Steven entered the room and paused in the doorway, his eyes scanning the table before resting on Theo. A muscle in his jaw clenched as he strode to the empty seat at the other end of the table. A barely audible sigh came out of Theo's lips. He'd hoped to reconcile with Steven today, but his brother's mood wasn't amicable.

The family closed their eyes and prayed silently to God, then began to eat their meal of fried chicken, mashed potatoes, and peas.

Theo savored the rich, satisfying taste of the fried chicken as he ate, relishing each bite and letting the flavors linger on his tongue. The tender, buttery potatoes were silky smooth against his tongue, while the salty sweetness of the peas was a perfect complement to it all. After all the bland food he'd endured numerous times in the military, food had become more than just fuel for Theo. It was an expression of love and care, a way for his family to show their support and affection for him. Eating this meal was like being wrapped in a warm embrace, and he felt his body and spirit relax as he enjoyed the simple comfort of his mother's cooking.

After dinner, Theo offered to clear the plates while Ivan and Linda went to their room. As he began to clear the plates from the table, Steven stared at him with a wary expression on his face. He seemed suspicious, as if he didn't trust his brother or his motives for helping out around the house. Theo felt a twinge of hurt and annoyance at how Steven was looking at him, but he tried to push those feelings aside.

Although he didn't like the strife between them, he knew their strained relationship was largely due to his time away in the military and their competition for Evelyn. He had responded to Steven's anger with aggressive competition the day he'd returned, and he wondered if he could amend that mistake. It had been so wrong of him to start their new relationship in such a negative way. Trying to heal the rift between them, he forced a smile and offered a tentative greeting, hoping to open up a line of communication between them, but Steven ignored him.

Theo sighed in exasperation and went to his room after dinner. He knelt by his bed and began to pray to God, "Lord, I know that there is strife between Steven and me. Please forgive me for how harsh and cruel I was to him. I don't know what to do about it, but I pray that you will help us to mend our relationship. I know it will take time, but I'm willing to do whatever it takes. Help me to discern your will and to make the right choices. If Evelyn is meant to be with me, and I pray she is, I ask that you would reveal that to her and show her what to do. Amen."

As Theo prayed, he felt peace begin to fill him. He knew that God was in control, and no matter what happened, he could trust Him. He also felt a prompting from the Holy Spirit to pray for Steven and Evelyn, but he couldn't bring himself to comply. He wasn't sure if God wanted him to pray for them individually or as a couple. Praying for them as a couple was a line he wouldn't cross.

At least, he now had a renewed sense of peace and determination.

Theo clasped his hands around his left ankle and slowly raised his leg, feeling the resistance as his muscles worked to lift his leg. He held the position for a few seconds before lowering his leg back to the starting position. He repeated the exercise, this time with his right leg, and then continued to alternate between the two legs.

The exercise routine had been part of his physical therapy. While it was slow going, he felt like his progress was encouraging. Although his leg would probably never be as strong as it was before the injury, he was determined to regain as much strength and mobility as possible.

Once he'd completed the leg exercises, he added some basic strength and core exercises and went to bed.

The next day, the family went to church. After the service, the celebration for Theo's return began. Members of the Amish community brought food and shook hands with him or hugged him. The delicious aroma of the food gave the place a festive atmosphere.

Theo was grateful for the warm welcome from his community. As he looked around at the smiling faces of his friends and neighbors, he felt a sense of belonging. He was reminded of what he'd been missing while in the Army, and he vowed never to take his Amish community for granted again.

"It's good to have you back, Theo," one of his friends said.

"I'm glad you're home," another added.

Theo smiled. Maybe, just maybe, things were finally going to start looking up. But a glance to the right made him see Steven frowning at him. Evelyn's parents had neutral expressions, although the awkwardness between them and Theo was still present. They shook his hands stiffly and went to the other end of the room. Livia watched him with narrowed, cautious eyes.

Theo sighed. He knew there was a lot of healing to do. His gaze roamed the church hall with a calculating look. He appraised the atmosphere like he would a battle. Who was on his side? Who needed a little more convincing, and who openly detested him?

At that moment, he found out something surprising. Several ladies in the hall were glancing at Steven covertly. The realization that his brother was a much sought-after bachelor despite being engaged dawned on him. Maybe if news of Theo wanting Evelyn had spread, the ladies saw Steven as a potential husband. He also recalled how Steven had many admirers when they were younger but had been oblivious. It was probably because he had his eyes only on Evelyn all along.

As he watched his brother interact with the community, Theo felt a renewed sense of determination and hope. He could find another befitting wife for Steven and get married to Evelyn. That would solve the problem amicably.

Theo noticed Evelyn glancing at him subtly out of the corner of his eye. Her gaze lingered on him for a moment, and he felt a flutter of excitement in his chest as he wondered what she was thinking. He kept his expression neutral so as not to betray his interest. Her gaze finally broke away from him.

Theo let out a breath he didn't realize he'd been holding. His heart was pounding in his chest, and he felt a strong urge to go over and talk to her. Standing up from his seat, he started to walk toward her.

But just as he took a step, Steven moved in Evelyn's direction. He gestured to her, and they began talking. Theo watched them for a moment, feeling annoyance and jealousy bubbling up inside him. He took another step towards them when Livia blocked his path, glaring.

"What do you think you're doing?" she asked in a low voice.

"I'm going to talk to Evelyn."

"You're going to leave her alone," she said in a warning tone.

"Livia, I'm not going to hurt her. I just want to talk."

"Theo, Steven loves Eve. He spent several years working hard to win her love."

Livia watched the couple with a mixture of adoration and protectiveness. Theo wondered what had elicited such feelings in her. At the same time, she seemed to resent him for his attention to Evelyn. Obviously, she saw him as a threat to the relationship between Steven and Eve.

"You need to consider *your brother's* feelings for once. So just leave her alone, all right?"

A spark of annoyance rose in Theo. "I know you're protective of them, but I don't need you to tell me what to do."

"Somebody needs to," she replied and stalked off.

He watched her go, feeling frustrated. He turned away and left the hall, deciding to talk to Evelyn some other time. He found some shade inside the buggy and watched on while the congregation started dispersing.

"Theo."

The soft voice of his mother made him turn.

"*Maem*," he said, inclining his head in respect.

"You've matured a lot since you joined the Army, but there's one important trait you need to work on," Linda said, joining him in the buggy.

"What's that?" Theo asked, his brow furrowed in confusion.

"Your selfishness," she said bluntly. "Despite understanding what it means to discard personal pleasures and serve your country, you're still thinking only about what you want and not about others."

Theo frowned. "That's not true."

"It is," she insisted. "You left your brother to join the Army. And now you're back, and you're trying to take Evelyn away from him."

"I'm not trying to take her away from him," he protested weakly.

"Then what were you trying to do?" a voice asked in his head.

"Your intentions might not be bad, but that doesn't change how your actions will affect your brother. The fact is, if you take Evelyn away from Steven, it will hurt him deeply. He's only just started to heal from when you left," she explained. "Do you know that Steven asked Evelyn about her feelings for you before asking to court her? It was only out of respect for you that he asked Evelyn if she had dated you. Perhaps he wouldn't have entered into a relationship with her if he hadn't understood that there had been nothing between the two of you."

Linda sighed as she looked at her son. "Theo, if you try to snatch Evelyn out of Steven's hands now that you've reappeared back unexpectedly, it will paint you in a negative light. You have told her you love her, so now you need to respect both your brother and Evelyn's feelings and let her make the decision about whether she wants to be with you or with him. It's up to her now."

Theo remained silent, digesting his mother's words.

"Plus, you should always think about how your actions will affect others before you do something. That's what it means to be unselfish," she said gently and left.

Theo didn't step down from the buggy as people milled about in front of the church, talking and laughing. His mother's words had penetrated to a soft spot he'd thought had hardened. His decision to marry Evelyn and Linda's advice were like two ropes dragging him to opposite ends.

Finally, with a clenched fist, he groaned.

"*Maem*," he whispered though no one was there, "What you ask of me is too difficult."

Chapter Twenty-two

Steven breathed a sigh of relief as the celebration for Theo's return finally ended later that afternoon at the church. People were chatting with each other outside the church, and Evelyn was talking to Laura. Luckily, Theo was nowhere to be seen, allowing Steven to bring down his guard.

Steven caught sight of Bishop Byler talking to two men and walked up to him. Steven regretted how he reacted to Theo. Such unbridled anger was disheartening and unbefitting even though Theo deserved it. He'd made up his mind to work on his anger, and he wasn't planning to change his mind.

"Good afternoon, Bishop Byler," he said once the bishop dismissed the two men, "can we talk somewhere more private?"

The bishop nodded and led him to a corner of the church. "How can I help you, Steven?"

"As you know, I've been struggling with my brother leaving us. I have to confess something. When my brother came back, I became angry and treated him harshly."

"It's only natural," Bishop Byler replied. "You were angry when he first left, and you're angry now that he's back."

"I know. I don't want to be, but I can't help it. What am I supposed to do? My parents forgave him, but I can't even bring myself to talk to him."

"Your parents forgave Theo because of biblical principles. Remember that Jesus asked us to forgive those who wrong us seventy times seven times," the bishop reminded him.

"But my brother didn't even ask for forgiveness," he huffed. "He just showed up one day and expected us to welcome him back with open arms."

"Do you remember the story of the prodigal son? The father welcomed his son home with open arms even though he had done wrong."

Steven's eyes darted away. Forgiving Theo was easier said than done.

"I know it's difficult," the bishop said as if reading his mind. "But you need to find it in your heart to forgive your brother. Otherwise, you'll never be able to move on."

Steven nodded.

Inside his mind, he was shaking his head. Theo rejoining his family came with lots of problems. Even though his brother had rejoined the community, Steven didn't want to be second to him. That was all he'd ever been when they were growing up, and he couldn't bear to take up that position now they were adults.

Only one thing could help Steven. Theo could move away from the farm, leaving Steven to manage the farm he'd rebuilt. To be fair, his brother probably got monetary benefits from the military and would hopefully still have money from the inheritance to buy land and start his own farm. This time around, Theo would truly be fulfilling the commitment he made six years ago to buy his own farm instead of deceiving them all and leaving the Amish community.

If Theo could fulfill this condition, then Steven wouldn't resent him for the pain he'd caused.

"Thank you, Bishop Byler," he said and left the church to get some fresh air.

He caught sight of Livia outside. She was scowling at Theo, who was sitting in a buggy. Remembering how helpful she had been in his courtship with Evelyn, he went to her, his feet treading lightly on the grass.

"Good afternoon, Livia," he said.

She looked up at him. "Hello, Steven."

"I wanted to thank you for your help in my courtship with Evelyn. If it hadn't been for you, I wouldn't have won her over."

She blushed and ducked her head. "It was nothing."

"No, it wasn't," he insisted. "You were a big help, and I'm very grateful."

Livia smiled at him, and her eyes lit up. She looked radiant when she smiled. "I'm glad I could help."

A thought that had been niggling at his mind came back to him, and he said, "Why did you stop visiting our farm after giving me such good advice about Evelyn? You advised me on the kind of gifts to give her for her birthday, then disappeared."

She frowned. "I didn't give you advice, Steven. You decided to implement everything we talked about."

"But I don't remember that. I remember talking to you about the gifts, and then, suddenly, you were gone."

Livia looked down at her hands. "I didn't want to overstep my bounds. I was only trying to help."

He shrugged. "That's alright. Well, I never got to personally thank you for helping out on the farm. Once Evelyn asked you to pitch in with the farm work, you agreed to without asking for anything in return."

"I asked Evelyn to help you on the farm, not the other way around," she said in a strange tone.

Steven stared at Livia in surprise. He'd never asked who had come up with the idea. Since Evelyn was his childhood friend, he'd assumed she'd been the one to think of it.

He gave Livia a second look, realizing that there was much more to her than he'd thought. She was intelligent and insightful, with a gentle personality that was very appealing yet fiercely protective of those she loved. Any man who would marry her would be lucky.

But then something else piqued his curiosity, so he asked, "Why did you ask Evelyn to help me? Yes, I needed the help. But you and I were not close when you organized your friend to pitch in. So, why did you do it?"

She hesitated for a moment, then looked at him with clear eyes.

"I wanted to help you because I care about you." Her eyes flicked away. "As a friend. I care about you as a friend. You and I are both Amish, and you needed help more than you've ever needed it. So, I did the first thing that came to my mind. It was only the right thing to do."

Steven was touched by her words. He'd never realized that she was this kind-hearted. "Thank you for your help. I appreciate it more than you know."

She smiled at him, and involuntarily, his lips turned up in a reflective smile.

"I'm glad I could help. I'll always be there for you if you need me."

Steven nodded, feeling a deep sense of gratitude towards Livia. She was a true friend, and he would always cherish her friendship. For now, he had Evelyn. But if Theo tried to take her away manipulatively, he could count on Livia to help him keep Eve by his side.

Chapter Twenty-three

Theo decided to honor his mother's wishes to stop competing with Steven over Evelyn. That meant he would stop trying to convince her to end her engagement to Steven, and if she chose to marry his brother anyway, he would have to see her being Steven's wife. It was already too painful for him to see them doing everything together on the farm. If Evelyn married Steven, he wasn't sure if he could stay here. It would break his parents' hearts, but he would have to leave again, though he didn't know where he would go.

Perhaps Evelyn was afraid Theo would leave again. Was that why she hadn't decided to be with him? If he bought a farm to show that he was staying, maybe she would see that he was just as responsible and dependable as Steven. Yes, that would show her how much he loved her.

Unfortunately, he didn't have much money left. Over the years, he'd squandered his share of the inheritance his father had given him. He'd never saved up while in the military, and after cutting off communication with Evelyn, he'd spent his money recklessly.

Although he would be getting veteran disability compensation monthly, the amount couldn't help him pay for the type of farmland he wanted. He had no choice but to ask his father for a job on the farm, or he could work somewhere else and earn more money quickly. On Monday morning, Theo went to speak to his father. Ivan was herding the animals with the other farmhands. There were the usual sounds of bleating, mooing, and the occasional neigh.

Theo joined his father to work. He noticed how Ivan's movements were slower. He didn't look as strong as when Theo had left to join the Army. Theo hadn't expected his father's strength to deteriorate so fast. Probably working alone with Steven just after he left had affected Ivan's health. Theo hung his head in regret, feeling guilty and responsible for the deterioration of his father's health, especially since his parents had been sick and he'd had no idea. Ivan and Steven must have struggled to keep the farm running smoothly without his help and making the loan payments.

What had he done to them? Yes, he'd served his country, but what price had his family paid because of it? How had he not realized it before?

"*Daed*, I need to ask you for a favor," Theo began.

"What is it, son?" Ivan replied.

Theo hesitated for a moment, looking down at the ground before meeting his father's gaze.

"I spent the inheritance that you gave me."

Ivan frowned, looking concerned. "What happened, Theo? How? What did you spend it on? Did something happen? Was it your medical bills?"

Theo shook his head.

"I gambled it away and bought an expensive car. I was so foolish. I lost it all. I didn't save anything while I was in the Army," he said slowly. "I'm sorry, *Daed*. I know how you took a loan to get the money."

"I made poor financial decisions. I let my desires overwhelm my common sense." He took a deep breath and continued. "To be honest, I want to buy farmland and build a new home here, but I don't have enough money. I was hoping I could ask for a job on the farm."

His father sighed. "You don't have to ask, Theo. I'm your *daed* and would never refuse such a thing from you."

Theo smiled, understanding.

"Come on," Ivan said, gesturing to him to come towards the sheep. "I'm putting you in charge of the sheep. You excelled in that area if I remember clearly. You'll need to make sure the fences are mended and that there's food and water for the sheep. You'll also need to check their feet regularly and shear them when necessary."

Theo nodded, understanding his father's instructions. He knew how to take care of sheep from when he was younger. Ivan had taught him the basics.

"I'll take good care of them, *Daed*. I promise. I won't waste this opportunity. I'll work hard and make you proud of me again."

Ivan smiled at him fondly and patted his shoulder affectionately. Theo's heart swelled with gratitude toward him.

His *daed* would surely give him a fair wage. Then he could save up his veteran benefits, get a loan, and buy farmland. That would make the members of the Amish community finally view him as honorable, and he could live out his days in peace and quiet even though he'd never get married to Evelyn. A pang of sadness hit his chest at the thought. He thrust it out before it overwhelmed him. Before coming back to Unity, he'd known things wouldn't be so easy. But at least now he had a chance to start fresh.

Theo worked hard on the farm that day, doing what he could despite his injured leg, determined to make up for lost time. Everyone was amiable except for Steven, who only gave him polite nods and curt replies. It was a far cry from the brother he had grown up with who had laughed with him and played with him when they were younger.

As afternoon turned to dusk and the sunlight dimmed, Theo told the workers to go home, and he herded the animals into the barn. He looked up to see Evelyn approaching in her buggy.

His heart skipped a beat at the beauty and grace that encompassed her. Feelings of longing and desire flooded his heart as he watched her. He reminded himself belatedly that she was betrothed to his brother. He looked around quickly. Steven wasn't in the field, and his parents were in the farmhouse.

Before Evelyn could see his reaction to her, Theo went into the barn to take care of the sheep. He switched on the battery-operated lanterns, fed them, and checked them over.

A few minutes later, Evelyn's silhouette fell across the barn doorway. Theo didn't need to look up to know it was her. She had the scent of flowers, and her presence arrested his attention.

"Good evening, Theo. Have you seen Steven? I can't find him in the fields or in the farmhouse, and your *daed* said I should ask you if you've seen him around."

Her voice was soothing, like a cool breeze on a hot day. It made him feel at ease. Theo stopped himself from sighing at his love for her flaring up within him.

"I don't know where he is. Maybe he left the farm to run errands," he said instead.

She stepped into the barn and pointed to his outstretched injured leg. "How is your leg? Have you seen a doctor since you came back?"

He shook his head. "No, I'm fine. It's much better. I underwent physical therapy after the injury."

"Theo," she scolded softly. "You shouldn't lie to me. I can see the pain in your eyes."

He looked away quickly, not wanting her to see the truth in his eyes. He didn't want her to know how much he was hurting inside, not just physically but emotionally as well.

"Please go see a doctor," she implored quietly. "If not for yourself, then do it for me. I worry about you."

Her words penetrated through the fog of pain. She stared at him with soulful eyes.

"I wish you'd never stopped writing letters to me. What happened after we stopped exchanging letters? Did you start dating another woman?" she asked.

He chuckled. "No, Eve. It's always been you."

"Then what happened?"

"I focused on serving the Army on the frontlines." He paused, wondering if telling her about his PTSD was wise. "I felt stained and unworthy. I didn't want to disturb you anymore, and I felt I deserved to be in pain after my actions."

"But weren't there times when you almost lost your life? Did you not think of me then?" she asked, sounding hurt.

Theo's heart ached at the thought of how much he'd hurt her. "I thought of you all the time, Eve. You were my reason for living, my reason to keep going when things got tough."

"Then why didn't you come back to me? Why didn't you write to me?" she asked, her voice trembling.

"I'm sorry," he choked out. "I love you, but I thought since we didn't have a future together, it would be better to put distance between us."

"Theo," she cried and gently touched his arm.

"I want you to know I'm going to buy farm land here in Unity. I'm going to stay here for good," he told her. "I just thought you should know."

"Oh, Theo. You're staying?"

He nodded.

"I was so worried you'd leave again." She took a step closer to him. "I love you so much. I…"

His hand moved of its own accord, holding her hand and enveloping it. Her words cut abruptly short, and she gazed at him longingly. His skin began to tingle where they touched. Suddenly, Theo was aware of his heart pounding in his chest.

They were in the barn alone. Nobody would see if he kissed her.

A strong impulse to give in to temptation settled in his mind. He tried to shake it away. He'd promised his mother and prayed about it. He ought to tell Evelyn to leave before he did something he would later regret.

Instead, he spoke with a hoarse voice, "Eve, may I kiss you?"

Her eyes turned doubtful. A kiss would escalate to other things, wouldn't it?

It wouldn't, his mind argued. *It's just one kiss to remember my Eve by for the rest of my life.*

Or would it haunt him for the rest of his life?

He stood up, balancing on his good leg. He drew closer to her. "Please, kiss me just this once. I'll cherish the memory forever in my heart. I won't tell a soul."

Theo's heart ached for her as she stared up at him, and he gently touched her face. Her hands tentatively touched his arms, roaming over the muscles in his shoulders. He wrapped his hands around her waist, pulling her close to him. She was so close that he could almost hear her heart pounding, just as his was. She wrapped her arms around him as they clung to each other, then she lifted her chin, closing her eyes. As he bent his head lower to meet her waiting lips, a shuffling sound made him stiffen. A sheep bleated loudly.

Theo and Evelyn turned. Steven's wide eyes stared at them from a stall.

Theo and Evelyn sprung apart like a tightly drawn string that had been cut.

Steven! He must have fallen asleep in a stall, Theo thought, recalling that his brother had formed the habit of sleeping in the barn in the afternoons when they were teenagers.

Evelyn's mouth was wide open in horror.

"Steven," she finally squeaked out and rushed to him.

Theo felt a rush of adrenaline and shame. A mixture of guilt and regret over his actions reverberated in his chest. He stood frozen, unable to look away from his brother's wide, questioning eyes.

"Steven, I can explain," Evelyn said as she hurried over to him.

But Steven wasn't looking at her. His face was red with anger as he glared at Theo. His fists were clenched at his sides, and he looked like he was about to explode, maybe even hit his brother.

"Steven, please." Evelyn's hand reached out to him, her heart wrenching at the look on his face.

He lifted his hand, signaling her not to come any closer. He stomped out of the barn, then Evelyn looked from Theo to the door.

"Go after him," Theo said, suddenly feigning interest in watching the sheep. "He's your fiancé. He might listen to you."

Evelyn hesitated for a moment, but when she left, he felt an aching emptiness in his chest. Theo sat down on a stool, shoulders drooping. He could still feel her close to him, in his arms, pressed against his chest. If only a moment more had passed between them, they would have kissed.

How would he feel now if they actually had? He already felt guilty enough.

It was already getting dark outside as the sheep grew restless, shuffling their feet and bleating. Those close to him rubbed their bodies on his leg, but Theo was oblivious to his surroundings.

He'd acted on his attraction for Evelyn despite knowing it was wrong. He should have fought against his feelings instead of giving in to them. At that moment, he knew that he'd betrayed his mother's trust and his own values, and he felt deeply regretful for what he had done. Theo wished he could turn back time and undo his actions, but it was too late. Evelyn's fiancé, his brother, had witnessed his indiscretion, and nothing could change that now.

Theo had thought he could work on the farm until he saved enough money to buy land, but now he realized that would be impossible. His longing for Evelyn, especially now that he knew he couldn't have her, had turned to an overwhelming ache. It made him act irrationally.

With a heavy heart, he determined that there was only one solution for him. He needed to leave the farm and find a job that would take up all his time, so he'd leave for his job early in the morning and come back at night, but he wouldn't be able to avoid seeing her at church. He would also have to fast-track getting a loan to buy another farm so he could move away. Then he could be far away from Evelyn and his desire for her.

Even now, his senses chafed at that idea. His memory was savoring every moment he'd shared with Eve. Theo had no choice. To stay true to himself, taking quick action and leaving Unity as soon as he could was a sacrifice he had to make, even if he broke his parents' hearts all over again.

And Evelyn's.

Chapter Twenty-four

After Evelyn's encounter with Theo in the barn, guilt descended on her like a hammer of judgment as she rode back home. The image of her almost kissing Theo repeated in her mind, reminding her that what she had done was wrong.

A shiver ran through her body as she realized the true meaning of her actions. Not only was she engaged, but she was also Amish. In the eyes of her community, she'd committed sexual immorality, and she felt guilty and ashamed. She knew that such thoughts and feelings would continue to plague her even after she married Steven because, deep down, she was still in love with his brother, and now she knew that would never change.

This was wrong, so very wrong, and yet she couldn't help the way she felt.

Evelyn knew that she needed to confess her sins and ask for forgiveness. But first, she had to come to terms with the fact that her attraction to Theo was something she'd have to battle for the rest of her life if she married Steven.

But what if she ended the engagement with Steven? Hope stirred up in her heart, followed by gloom; it would hurt him more. Plus, she'd need to stop the wedding preparations.

She'd have to tell the bishop they were no longer getting married and send mail to her relations in Lancaster and Smyrna to tell them the wedding was canceled. It would be so shameful to announce that she had canceled her wedding, yet it was better to end things now than to live a lie.

Despite her conflicted feelings, she had to do what was best for both herself and Steven. She couldn't continue dragging out their engagement if she wasn't truly committed to the relationship. But at the same time, she didn't want to cause Steven any further pain or heartbreak by ending things abruptly.

Evelyn had a lot of thinking and soul-searching to do. Whatever decision she ended up making, she needed to be honest with herself and Steven about her feelings for Theo. And if there was no hope for a future between them, she'd have to let Theo go.

As she struggled with her decision, she turned to God for guidance. She sought the Lord's forgiveness for her mistakes and prayed that He'd guide her on the difficult task ahead and show her the right path forward.

With a heavy heart, she made her way back home. She resolved to stay away from Theo to resist the temptation of giving in to her feelings for him. There was only one way to do that. She had to stop going to the farm.

Days later, Livia visited Evelyn to talk about the wedding. Evelyn couldn't concentrate throughout her friend's one-sided boisterous conversation in the living room. All she could think of was how she was getting married to the wrong brother. Finally, she decided to pour out her feelings as they sat on the couch together.

"I don't think I can go through with the wedding," she said, trying to be firm. But her voice shook at the tail end of the sentence.

Livia gave her a resigned look, a frown marring her forehead.

Evelyn stared at the floor as she continued, "I know I'm supposed to love Steven, but Theo makes me feel alive and passionate, things that I don't experience with his brother. With Theo, I feel like I can be myself. He accepts me for who I am. He makes me feel relaxed, and we have this easy connection that I can't explain. I've had feelings for him for so long; I can't deny that there's something deeper between us."

"Have you talked to Steven about this?" Livia asked.

She shook her head. "No, I don't know how to tell him."

"This is a difficult situation, but I think you need to be honest with Steven. He deserves to know how you feel," Livia said.

Evelyn was shocked at the response. She'd thought Livia would get angry like the last time, but her friend was calmly listening to her and could be considering siding with her.

"I'm scared of hurting him," she admitted.

"It's better to hurt him now than to keep hurting him later on," Livia said gently. "If you marry him without telling him how you feel about Theo, it will only make things worse for both of you. So, it's better you break off the engagement right now."

Evelyn stared at her friend in disbelief. "Are you sure?"

"Yes," she said firmly. "Steven deserves to have someone who truly loves him, and if that's not going to be you, then he should find someone else."

"What...what made you change your mind? A few days ago, you told me I should remain committed to Steven."

Livia's body stiffened. A blush that was getting redder by the second formed on her cheeks. Evelyn looked at her in shock as she realized that she'd been missing an important detail of her friend's life.

"Livia, what's going on?"

"Nothing." Livia crossed her arms.

"Do you have feelings for Steven?" A wide grin spread across Evelyn's face. How could she have not seen it until now?

"Yes," Livia whispered, staring at the floor.

"Why didn't you tell me? You could have told me," Evelyn said, grabbing her hand as sadness for her friend filled her. "It must have been so hard for you to see him with me. I'm so sorry, Livia. I had no idea. If I knew, I never would have said yes to him. You're my best friend."

Her friend's face was flushed as she stammered out an explanation. "To be honest, I've always been in love with Steven, but I never acted on it because I didn't want to come between him and you. I knew he loved you and didn't want to ruin your relationship."

"Why didn't you just tell me?"

"I was afraid of losing your friendship. I didn't want to lose the only person who truly understands me."

"Oh, Livia," Evelyn murmured, throwing her arms around her friend as tears pricked her eyes. "But then why did you encourage the idea of Steven courting me?"

"I love you both so much. I just wanted the two of you to be happy," Livia said, her voice cracking, then a sob escaped her lips. Livia's chest shuddered as Evelyn held her. "Like when I suggested we go help Steven at the farm, I did it because I love him. When I saw how much he was in love with you, I made up my mind to get the two of you together. The two of you being happy is more important to me than my own feelings."

"But Steven and I are clearly not meant to be, Livia. You made so many sacrifices for me, and I had no idea. I feel like such an awful friend," Evelyn choked out, pulling away as she put a hand over her heart, which was breaking for her friend.

"You're the best friend I've ever had, Evelyn. I was prepared to see you marry the man I love rather than risk ruining our friendship."

Now Evelyn burst into tears, and the two women hugged once more as they cried on each other's shoulders.

Deep down, Evelyn had always known that her feelings for Steven were superficial. She'd never truly connected with him, never felt the spark of passion or excitement she felt with Theo.

Yet she hadn't noticed Livia's love for him.

"I'm so ashamed of how selfish and thoughtless I've been, ignoring your feelings in pursuit of my own. How could I not see it? If I'd focused on others instead of only on myself, you and Steven might be engaged at the moment. Now, instead, I'm about to break his heart, and this all could have been prevented. I'm such a fool," Evelyn said, wiping her eyes and leaning back on the couch.

"You're not a fool, Evelyn. He barely noticed me and only had eyes for you. I tried to get his attention," Livia said quietly. "I tried to make him see me, but all he saw was you. He only ever talked about you when he was with me. When I told him what you and I liked for birthday gifts, he bought all the gifts for you. When I asked you to help him out on the farm with me, he thought his Evelyn had come up with the idea. Besides taking care of his family, Steven's only goal was to win your heart and love. I couldn't take that away from him, so I stopped visiting him after he bought the flowers and books for your birthday. I decided that if I couldn't have him, then let him have a good woman by his side as his wife. He deserves that."

"I didn't know. I should have known because we're friends." Evelyn chuckled and shook her head. "I've been hogging the good guys, haven't I? Theo and Steven."

Livia's lips turned up in a smile.

Evelyn began to think up ways she could facilitate a match between Steven and Livia. It would be the best solution for everyone if she could make Steven see that Livia was a much better match for him that Evelyn ever was. That way, Steven would be happy and fulfilled instead of heartbroken and miserable like he'd be when she broke off the engagement. And Evelyn would have her chance to marry Theo – the man she truly loved and desired.

"You're the answer to my prayers, Livia," Evelyn said. "I'm going to do everything I can to make Steven realize how wonderful you are and get the two of you together."

"Thank you, Evelyn." Livia beamed. "That would be my answer to prayer, even after I thought it was impossible."

Evelyn smiled, feeling a sense of peace and understanding wash over her. For the first time in a long while, she was truly hopeful that everything would turn out right in the end.

The next day, Steven picked up Evelyn from the bookstore to take her home. She knew why he'd come. He wanted to speak to her about what had happened in the barn. Her heart went out to him. Steven was a good man. It wouldn't be fair to him to keep putting him in situations leading to despair.

Evelyn got into the buggy. The atmosphere was heavy. An oppressing, stifling silence reminded her of how she'd flirted with Theo. She decided to wait till they got to her house.

When they drove into her yard, Steven turned to her. "Evelyn, about what happened—"

"Steven, I need to tell you something," she interrupted.

He crossed his arms over his chest. "Go ahead."

"I..." She hesitated for a few seconds, then forced herself to say the words that would end their courtship: "I can't marry you."

Steven's eyes widened in shock. "What? But why?"

"Because of Theo and what happened between us. I have always loved him, and that will never change. It would be so unfair for me to bring that into our marriage."

"Theo. Of course." He chuckled bitterly and shook his head. "That explains everything. You've said you love me several times, but your actions yesterday proved you've been lying all along. You were about to kiss."

She scooted away from him, scared of his reaction. "I didn't mean for things to get so out of hand."

"I saw the way you looked at him and how you clung to him like he was your only lifeline. You've never looked at me or touched me like that, not once." Anger burned in his eyes as he glared at her, his fists clenching with frustration and hurt. "I thought you loved me. But the moment Theo came back, you ran back to him."

"It wasn't like that, Steven," she said pleadingly. "I do love you, but like a brother. You will always be like a brother to me. That's why I can't marry you. It's just not right, and it's not fair to you. I'm so sorry. I never meant for this to happen. I've made terrible mistakes."

Evelyn felt a sharp pang on seeing the pain in his eyes. She didn't like Steven's extreme reaction, but she'd brought it upon herself. She breathed in slowly and tried her best to speak steadily.

"I'm so sorry, Steven," she repeated when he refused to speak.

Steven let out a cry of anger. He punched the side of the buggy and turned away from her, his shoulders sagging with frustration and sadness. As they pulled into her driveway and the buggy stopped, Evelyn jumped out and stepped back in fear. For a long moment, Steven was silent. Then he spoke again, his voice thick with emotion.

"You never loved me. All you ever wanted was to use me." He stared at her, his eyes filled with hurt. "I loved you, Eve. I still do. I wanted us to be husband and wife. But now I realize that you had a different motive. You were only courting me as a replacement for Theo. Whatever feelings you had for me was a selfish way to satisfy yourself."

Evelyn felt her heart shatter at the pain in his voice. She wished she could take back the hurt she'd caused him, but she knew it was too late.

"I never meant to hurt you. I never meant for any of this to happen." She sighed. "I'm sorry, Steven. I hope one day you can forgive me."

Steven ignored her and turned the buggy around, his face darkening with pain and fury.

A flood of relief washed over Evelyn. Her heart should ache with guilt since Steven had been so loving to her. But now that she'd ended their courtship, all she felt was a burden lifting from her. She felt confused about her reaction. She'd just done the most horrible thing in her life by potentially shattering Steven's happiness and dreams, yet she felt no remorse.

Deep down, she knew she felt better because she knew it would be worse to marry Steven when she loved his brother and not him.

Still, she couldn't court Theo and marry him in a heartbeat after jettisoning his brother. She would have to ensure Steven and Livia courted so they could all be happy. The courtship would also help Steven deal with his hurt. She'd have to get him and her friend together. It was the best option.

But her ex-fiancé was angry with her and wouldn't be open to her suggestions. He needed time.

A sudden thought came to her: *If I convince Theo to help me get them together, we'll sort out the problem together before getting married.*

Just then, she realized that Steven hadn't left the house. He'd parked his buggy and was walking toward her, his expression still livid.

"I was half asleep for most of the flirting that happened yesterday. I could hear snatches of your conversation, but my mind has been forcing me to forget it and forgive you. Now, I remember," he said in a low, menacing tone. "Theo instigated your breaking up with me. He told you he loved you and insisted on kissing you. I should have known that my prodigal brother wouldn't relent until he succeeded in snatching you away from me."

He stormed off, returned to the buggy, and drove away.

A sense of premonition hit Evelyn. Steven had reacted badly when she'd broken off their engagement; he would act far worse now that he blamed Theo for the canceled marriage.

She quickly hitched a horse to a buggy and drove out of the yard. She had to tell Theo about the turn of events and convince him to get Steven to court Livia. If she got to the Glicks' farm before Steven, she might stop a brawl that could turn into a lifelong hatred between the brothers.

Evelyn sat in the buggy, gripping the reins tightly as she rode through the countryside. Her heart raced with fear at the thought of what Steven would do next. He was angry and likely to act rashly, and she feared for both his safety and Theo's.

As she drew closer to his buggy, she strained her eyes to see his expression. She could sense the fury radiating from him, and she feared that he would act rashly at any moment.

As she approached his vehicle, Steven suddenly veered off his lane and raced past her at breakneck speed. She was relieved when he drove past the shortcut and raced home through the long route; he'd never liked taking that road. Evelyn veered off onto the uneven path that led straight to the farm. She urged her horse onward and arrived a few minutes later.

She leaped down from the buggy and looked around, fearing that Steven might have already arrived and started a fight with Theo.

"Theo!" she screamed, not caring how she was disrupting the community by shouting.

Chapter Twenty-five

Theo was grooming a horse by the side of the barn. He was running a brush along the horse's coat, taking care to be gentle. As he worked, he murmured soothing words to the animal, who seemed to be enjoying the attention. Every now and then, Theo would stop and give the horse an affectionate pat before continuing.

He heard Evelyn's voice screaming his name and walked out to the field.

Evelyn looked panicked as she rushed to him, her eyes searching his body for something he couldn't identify. Her face was creased with worry, and she trembled with fear. Theo looked around the farm. He couldn't perceive any danger. The only danger he could see was in front of him. *Evelyn.*

Her presence was overwhelming. Theo couldn't help but notice how beautiful Evelyn looked, even in her anxious state. Some of her blond curls were peeking out of her *kapp*. Her perfect features were enhanced by the glowing sunlight that bathed her face, making her look radiant and ethereal. He was entranced by the way she moved closer to him, with grace and elegance despite her obvious fear.

"Eve," he said and stepped back, not wanting a repeat of their embrace in the barn. "What's wrong?"

"Has Steven come back?" she asked, her eyes darting from side to side.

"No."

"Please, when he comes back, don't listen to his taunting. Be calm and walk away from him."

His eyebrows arched. "What are you talking about, Eve? You want me to walk away from my younger brother?"

"Don't let anything he does make you hate him. He's just..."

The sound of a buggy rumbling down the dirt lane made Theo look up to see Steven driving recklessly to stop in front of them. He jumped down.

Theo frowned at the sight of his brother. He'd avoided Steven since the recent incident with Evelyn in the barn. He usually went out in the mornings to look for a job and only came back in the late afternoons when Steven had already gone out or was resting from the day's work on the farm. In the evenings, he took his dinner up to his room to eat. It had only been a few days since Theo had seen his brother, but already Steven looked like he had aged years. There were dark circles under his eyes, and his face was gaunt and pale.

He stormed over to Theo and Evelyn, his eyes narrowing angrily at Theo.

"What's going on?" Theo coolly asked before Steven got to them. He was already shifting into a defensive position as much as his injured leg would allow him to.

Evelyn hesitated, her eyes darting from one brother to the next. She took a deep breath, as if steeling herself to speak, and turned to Theo. "I broke off the engagement."

"This is all your fault!" Steven glared at Theo as he approached him. "You always have to be in the middle of everything, don't you?"

"What are you talking about?" Theo asked, his brow furrowing in confusion.

"Don't play innocent with me," he spat. "I know how you've tried to take everything away from me. Do you think you can take another inheritance you don't deserve? You think you can take my place on the farm? And now you think you can have my fiancé?"

Theo's eyes hardened. "Steven, I was wrong to ask *Daed* for the inheritance, but Evelyn and I love each other. We never meant to hurt you."

"Don't think you can use that to stop me from saying what I need to say," he replied, his tone bitter and cold. "I know what you're up to, and I won't let you get away with it."

He grabbed Theo roughly on the shoulder and pushed him hard, then threw a punch at him. Theo's fight reflex kicked in, and all the defense tactics he'd learned in the Army came into play. With a look of disgust, he ducked out of the way, holding back the instinct to fight back. Steven tripped, sprawling onto the ground.

"I'm sorry, Steven. Please, let's not fight. Evelyn and I didn't mean to hurt you. We can't help that we're in love," Theo pleaded with his brother.

"You took everything from me!" Steven cried and lunged at Theo with a roar, throwing another punch. Theo defended himself, and they began to fight, viciously trading blows and rolling around in the field. Steven attacked him as though he wanted to kill him. Despite his desire to let peace reign, Theo wouldn't let his brother get the better of him. With his combat training, he could easily kill his brother if he wanted to, but of course, he held back, not wanting to hurt him any more than he already was.

From the corner of his eyes, he saw Evelyn off to the side, screaming at them to stop. "Stop, please! Fighting is not the Amish way! Stop!" Her eyes were wide with fear as she watched them grapple.

The farm workers watched in horror, and several of the men rushed over and tried to break up the fight, but it was no use—the two brothers barely even noticed them.

The fight lasted for several moments until their father came out of the farmhouse.

"Stop!" Ivan shouted, rushing over to them. "What is the meaning of this?"

Theo and Steven froze immediately, their eyes locked on each other. Theo stood up, breathing heavily as he glared at his brother. He picked up his crutch, placed it under his armpit, and leaned on it. They were both covered in dirt, their clothes were torn. Theo's lip was bleeding, and he could feel the bruises forming on his face and body. Steven staggered to his feet, his chest heaving with anger and exertion.

Evelyn's body was shaking uncontrollably, tears spilling from her eyes. She walked backward toward her buggy, a look of wild fear in her eyes.

Theo groaned in frustration. Now that the rush of anger had died down, he realized that he'd acted exactly the way Evelyn had begged him not to. She'd tried to warn him. He got to the buggy just as she entered and held the horse's reins.

"I shouldn't have fought him. I should have listened to you. I'm so sorry, Evelyn."

A flash of disappointment crossed her face. She turned and looked stiffly ahead. "I came to tell you that Livia is in love with Steven. We'll be going to a Singing tomorrow, and I was hoping you and I could get them to start courting so Steven would be happy. But with all the violence I just witnessed, I'm not sure if he'll be a good fit for Livia or if you'll be a good fit for me."

Theo felt a deep sense of regret as Evelyn rode away from the farm, her face set in determination. He'd let his anger and frustration get the better of him, causing him to lash out at his brother in a completely unacceptable way. He'd let himself, his family, and the love of his life down.

As he made his way back to Ivan and Steven, he could feel his father's eyes on him.

"I'm disappointed in both of you," Ivan said, his voice ringing out loudly in the field. He looked around at the workers. "I'm sorry you witnessed this fight. But most of all, I didn't expect this brawl from my two sons, Theo and Steven. As your father, I didn't train you this way."

"He attacked me," Theo said. "I was just defending myself! He tried to punch me twice before I fought back."

"You're the one who started it," Steven growled. "You've been trying to break up the relationship between Evelyn and me since you arrived."

Ivan shook his head in disgust.

"I expected more from both of you," he said sternly. "Steven, you've stayed here in the Amish community and know our ways. You know better than to resort to violence. You need to learn to control your anger."

Steven began to protest, then shut his mouth and hung his head in shame.

"Theo, you've been in the Army and seen a lot of violence. You told me you were tired of the violence. Yet, you went back to fighting once you had a misunderstanding with your brother. You're the older brother. You should be setting a better example for Steven."

Theo and Steven stood silently, their eyes downcast.

"I'm sorry, *Daed*," Steven said in a barely audible voice.

Theo hung his head. He knew he deserved the words of rebuke. His thoughts went to Evelyn and how she'd looked at him with dismay. If he wasn't careful, he'd be branded as a violent person and would end up losing his Eve.

"I'm sorry, *Daed*," Theo said, looking up at his father's face. "It won't happen again."

"It better not. Now go tend to your injuries and ensure you make peace with one another."

Ivan turned and walked back into the farmhouse.

Chapter Twenty-six

Long after Ivan's reprimand, Steven lay on his bed thinking about his father's words. He'd fought with Theo despite his desire to show him the Amish way and how to live a life devoted to God. He'd allowed his anger to control him. It was a bitter pill to swallow. Steven had always wanted his father's approval, and once he had it, he'd lost it by letting his emotions get the best of him.

He felt ashamed. As he lay there wallowing in self-pity, he heard a knock on his door—four light taps spaced rhythmically. It was a knocking system he and Theo had used in childhood. He opened the door.

"It's a beautiful night. The moon is out, and we can talk outside," Theo said with a too-bright smile in the doorway.

Steven frowned.

His brother sighed. "Can we talk outside? I know you'd prefer not to have anything to do with me now, but just hear me out. After that, you can choose to reconcile with me or not."

Steven closed his eyes in thought. If he was to show Theo the biblical way, he had to at least listen to him. Reluctantly, he went with him.

When they got to the field, the moon illuminated the yard and cast shadows. Crickets chirped, and the cool night air calmed Steven's nerves. He sat down on a bench under a tree shade and turned to Theo.

"I'm listening," he said.

"I apologize for flirting with Evelyn and almost kissing her even though she was your fiancée. I acted arrogantly, and I truly regret lashing out at you when I first arrived. I'm also sorry for fighting you and everything else I've done wrong. I also abandoned you when I left years ago and should have known better than to leave the community without a thought for your feelings. I'm so sorry, Steven. I've been a fool."

Steven took a deep breath and nodded. His brother had done the unexpected—he'd said sorry first. "I appreciate your apology. It takes a lot of courage and humility to admit when you've made a mistake. I forgive you, Theo. I'm sorry, too, for letting my anger get the best of me. We've both made mistakes, but we can learn from them and become better people. I'm sorry I fought you and treated you so harshly, too."

Theo smiled at him gratefully. "I forgive you, Steven. I know this is difficult for you, but I'm grateful you're willing to try and repair our relationship."

Steven shrugged, trying not to let his emotions show on his face. "It's what God would want us to do," he said simply. "I forgive you too, my brother."

"Thank you, Steven. That means so much to me, really," Theo said.

Steven noticed a tear falling from Theo's eye. "I thought maybe our relationship would be ruined after that fight. I thought we might hate each other forever."

Theo threw his arms around Steven. "That's impossible. We're brothers. No matter how stupid we act, we will always love and forgive each other. Right?"

"Right." Steven pulled away and nodded, wiping his eyes.

"I will do everything I can to support you and make our relationship strong again," Theo said sincerely, then a familiar mischievous smile played on his lips. "You know, you throw a pretty good punch. I was surprised."

The two brothers chuckled, and for a moment, they felt as close as they had once been when they were children, before the cares of the world had weighed them down and caused them to drift apart.

Steven smiled gratefully at his brother, feeling a weight lifted off him. They were still brothers, no matter how much they'd changed. He was glad that he could now forgive and move on in peace. He picked up some small pebbles and tossed them across the yard, working off his nervous energy. He turned them over in his hand, feeling their coolness against his skin.

"I thought that Evelyn had fallen in love with me until you came back, and I saw how she looked at you with so much love. She'd never looked at me that way, which infuriated me." He shrugged. "Now I realize it's because she never loved me, not like she loves you. You've always gotten Evelyn's attention. Even when we were younger, she gravitated toward you, and I was overlooked. I was always jealous of that."

Theo's face was contemplative. "Maybe that's true. Besides Eve, many ladies admire you and think you'll make a good husband. I saw some of them glancing at you shyly during the celebration."

Steven glanced at him in surprise. "Really? I had no idea that anyone was interested in me like that."

Theo nodded. "Yes, it's true. You're a handsome and kind man, and many women see that. If you hadn't been so focused on Evelyn, you might have noticed that other ladies were interested in you."

Steven was silent for a moment, digesting this new information. "Thank you for telling me. It means a lot to know that other women might be interested in me. I never even knew it was a possibility."

"Aren't you interested in knowing who they are?" he asked with a mischievous twinkle in his eyes. "There's one person I can recommend. She's quite protective of you and Evelyn."

"Who?"

"Nah." Theo tsked and wagged his fingers. "You have to figure it all out by yourself."

Steven let out an exasperated sigh. "At least give me a clue."

Theo smirked. "I should keep you guessing, but I tend to be a benevolent brother. She's Evelyn's close friend."

Steven peered at Theo intently, wondering who he was talking about. Images of Livia came unbidden into his mind. He'd always asked her about Evelyn without bothering to find out how she was doing herself. Livia had always been there for him, helping him try to win Evelyn's heart. Then he remembered the way Livia had looked outside the church when he'd realized she had been with the one with the idea to help on the farm. It had been as if he were seeing her for the first time, and he noticed how beautiful, kind, and self-sacrificing she was. The thought made him sit straight up.

"Livia," he said in a soft tone as shock washed over him. "It must have been so hard for her all this time to see me chasing after Evelyn instead of her. She even encouraged it. Why did she do that?"

"She wanted the two of you to be happy. She's feisty, but she's selfless." Theo's smirk had turned into a grin. "You have feelings for her, too."

"No, I appreciate her. I didn't realize she felt that way. She's been a good friend to me."

At Theo's persistent grin, Steven let out an exasperated sigh. His brother wouldn't relent until he told him everything about his friendship with Livia.

"She helped me get Evelyn to agree to marry me. She's selfless, kind, and gentle. Any man who marries her will be lucky," Steven said.

"You can be that man if you go to the Singing tomorrow and ask her if you can drive her home in your buggy," Theo said with triumph. "She'll be there."

After that, they talked until the late hours of the night. Theo told Steven how Evelyn had told him about Livia. Then they went to their rooms to catch a few hours of sleep.

Steven didn't sleep, though. He kept tossing and turning in bed. He was glad that he and Theo had forgiven each other and they didn't have any more angry feelings between them, but he still needed to ask God for forgiveness. He'd behaved rashly and wanted to always act in line with God's word and the Amish doctrine. He took a deep breath and slowly exhaled.

"Father, forgive me for acting in anger and fighting with Theo. I should have put my trust in You and not let an angry thought enter my head. Help me to control my emotions more and to keep having a good relationship with Theo. In Jesus' name, amen," he whispered as the sun came up.

He recounted the Bible verses the bishop had given him to help him with his bursts of anger, taking in the words and letting their power calm his spirit. As he recited them, he felt his body relax, the tension dissipating from his mind.

His thoughts went to Livia. Could he really have a chance with her after never noticing her feelings toward him for several years? She'd stopped visiting him at the farm some time ago. He didn't blame her, realizing now that he'd bought the birthday gifts she'd mentioned for Evelyn.

He realized now that Eve was never truly his. They'd never been in love. It was better to focus on someone with whom he could build a relationship filled with love than to wallow in self-pity because of Evelyn, who had given her heart to his brother long ago.

Steven felt that Livia was everything a man could ever want in a wife. She was beautiful, kind, and loving. She'd even helped rebuild the farm by helping him, something that hadn't occurred to Evelyn, who had been closer to him. But he had to find out for himself. He had to find out what she felt instead of relying on Theo's account. Then, he'd see if their relationship could become more than friendship.

With a plan now in place, he decided that Theo was right. He would go to the Singing tomorrow and try to talk to Livia. He didn't know her well despite their acquaintance throughout the years and would have to start with being friends. Then maybe, just maybe, he would finally have a chance at love.

Steven became determined to find a way to talk to Livia. He worked throughout the day, whistling, smiling, and getting teased mercilessly by Theo. Steven tried his best to ignore him. His brother was incorrigible in his mischief.

After the day's work on the farm, he washed up and dressed quickly in his finest clothes, then headed to the singing with Theo. It seemed like all the young single people were there, chatting loudly and eating sweet and savory treats while they waited for it to begin. Evelyn and Laura talked animatedly with a few friends, but Steven couldn't see Livia anywhere. He was about to give up when he saw her sitting on a bench by herself, scribbling in a notebook. He hesitated for a moment, wondering how she would react if he approached her. But then he reminded himself that showing courage would put him in a positive light. He walked up to her and sat next to her on the bench.

"Hi, Livia. I'm glad you came," he said softly.

She looked up at him in surprise, her cheeks flushing pink. "Um, hi, Steven. I... I'm glad you're here, too."

He smiled at her and took a deep breath. He knew this was his chance.

"Livia," he said earnestly, "I've been thinking about the conversation we had outside the church on the day of Theo's celebration."

Her eyes lit up with hope.

"I'd like us to be close friends."

Her eyes dimmed.

His brows furrowed in confusion. "Did I say something wrong?"

She shook her head and looked away. "It's just that I hoped..." She trailed off and became quiet. "Never mind."

Steven's eyes searched for his brother to silently ask for help, but Theo was already talking to Evelyn. He turned back to Livia, reading disappointment all over her features. Then it dawned on him. She wouldn't want just friendship if she'd liked him for so long.

"If things go well, we won't have to stop at friendship. If you want, after we get to know each other better, we can court. It's just that I've realized I don't know you as well as I thought I did, despite the numerous discussions we've had. I want to know about you, to understand you..."

He stopped, not knowing how to say he wanted to see if they could love each other equally. But Livia was staring at him with wide, hopeful eyes. Then she smiled.

"Yes, let's start with being genuine friends," she whispered. "I want to get to know you better too. Let's see where it takes us."

When no one was looking, he grabbed Livia's hand and squeezed it gently. When his hand touched hers, sparks of electricity shot up his arm, straight to his heart, which began pounding wildly. His breath hitched when he met her eyes again, which were so deep and suddenly mysterious.

He'd never felt like this when he was with Evelyn—not even close.

How had he been so blind? How had he not realized before that what he was looking for had been right there the entire time?

Chapter Twenty-seven

Evelyn was delighted to see Steven drive Livia home in his buggy after the Singing ended. Now Evelyn walked home with Theo, enjoying the feel of the evening air.

She hadn't liked the violence between Theo and Steven. She'd wanted to avoid Theo, but he'd taken her breath away once he arrived at the singing with his brother. She'd noticed then how friendly they'd become, how he waited for Steven to talk to Livia before coming over to her. When he'd asked her to go for a short walk and Laura had kept nudging her on her ribs, she'd accepted.

It wouldn't hurt to give him one more chance. I love him, she'd thought then.

Now, butterflies fluttered in her stomach as they stopped on the dirt lane. Theo's gaze on her was steady, making her heart pound with excitement.

He took a deep breath and said, "Evelyn, I know things have been difficult between us lately. I'm so sorry for all the terrible mistakes I've made, and I want you to know that Steven and I have reconciled our relationship."

"That's so good to hear," Evelyn said in relief. "I'm so glad you've forgiven each other."

Theo nodded, then took her hands tenderly. "I care deeply for you. I love you. I have always loved you. I don't think I've ever lived a day of my life where I didn't love you, even when we were children. You are the woman of my dreams—kind, funny, smart, strong, and beautiful. I want to spend the rest of my life with you. I don't want to waste any more time without you. Will you marry me, Evelyn?"

Evelyn felt a surge of joy at Theo's declaration of love, her heart swelling with affection. Tears welled up in her eyes. Now that Steven and Livia had found each other, she was ready to court the love of her life. She cherished Theo's warmth and passion and loved him just as deeply. She quickly nodded her head in agreement and buried her face in her palms, a sudden shyness coming over her.

"Yes," she whispered breathlessly. "I'll marry you, Theo."

After a year, Evelyn finally married Theo, the man of her dreams, that following November. He had taken a year to save money, buy his own farm, and build their home.

Steven and Livia got to know each other better while courting for six months and then getting engaged. It was a double celebration as they were married on the same day as Evelyn and Theo.

Theo's parents and Evelyn's family were there to witness the special day. The entire Amish community in Maine also attended the wedding, and so did Evelyn's relations from Lancaster, Pennsylvania, and their sister community in Smyrna, Maine. Although Theo had retired from the Army, some of his former colleagues also made it to the wedding to show their support. Sergeant Ethan Mills, the *Englisher* who introduced him to the military, was also present at the wedding as his friend. Theo wished his good friend Justin could have been there to share his happiness, but he didn't let it taint his joy.

It was a beautiful day filled with love and delight. Evelyn looked forward to a happy life together with Theo. She was also happy that Livia would be married to her brother-in-law and childhood friend, Steven.

Now that Theo had gotten his own farm, he had built a home for them with the help of his family and the community, as was customary in Unity. Steven and Livia had promised to come over and help them finish establishing the farm, so she'd be seeing them often. Her brothers and many members of the community had also offered to pitch in to help. This was what Evelyn had always enjoyed about the Amish. They supported and loved each other. She was grateful to have such a huge family.

Ivan and Linda had already passed down their farm to Steven, but now that Steven had Livia's help running the farm, Ivan and Linda officially retired and moved into a smaller apartment that had been built on the side of the house. Everyone had been blessed with the desires of their hearts, and Evelyn was grateful to see everyone happy.

As they stepped out of the church on their wedding day, Theo took her hand in his and gave her a look filled with love.

"Evelyn, several years ago, I joined the Army to get a medal of honor and make myself feel important. I didn't do it to serve my country as my comrades did, but to serve myself.

I wanted to fill a void in my heart and make myself feel important. Now I see that void was where God was missing in my life. I did it without thinking of the consequences of my actions or how it would affect those I loved. But in the end, God, love, and family matter the most. I'm grateful to have you by my side as my wife. You've made me the happiest man alive. You're so beautiful, and I love you."

Evelyn smiled back at him, feeling grateful for Theo and their love. "I love you too, Theo. I always will, forever."

"Forever," Theo replied as he picked her up in his arms. She laughed as he carefully set her on the seat of the buggy, not caring if anyone saw them. He climbed into the driver's seat, and they made their way to their new home, where they would build their life together.

About the Author (Ashley Emma)

Visit www.AshleyEmmaAuthor.com to download free eBooks by Ashley Emma!

Ashley Emma wrote her first novel at age 12 and published it at 16. She was home schooled and knew since she was a child that she wanted to be a novelist. She's written over 20 books and is now an award-winning USA Today bestselling author of over 15 books, mostly Amish fiction. (Many more titles coming soon!)

Ashley has a deep respect and love for the Amish and wanted to make sure her Amish books were genuine. When she was 20, she stayed with three Amish families in a community in Maine where she made many friends and did her research for her Amish books. To read about what it was like to live among the Amish, check out her book Amish for a Week (a true story).

Ashley's novel Amish Alias was a Gold Medal Winner in the NYC Book Awards 2021. Her bestselling book Undercover Amish received 26 out of 27 points as a finalist in the Maine Romance Writers Strut Your Stuff novel writing competition in 2015. Its sequel Amish Under Fire was a semi-finalist in Harlequin's So You Think You Can Write novel writing competition also in 2015. Two of her short stories have been published online in writing contests and she co-wrote an article for ProofreadAnywhere.com in 2016. She judged the Fifth Anniversary Writing Contest for Becoming Writer in the summer of 2016.

Ashley owns Fearless Publishing House in Maine where she lives with her husband and four children. She is passionate about helping her clients self-publish their own books so they can build their businesses or achieve their dream of becoming an author.

Download some of Ashley's free Amish books at www.AshleyEmmaAuthor.com.

ashley@ashleyemmaauthor.com

>>>>Check out Ashley's TV interview with News Center 6 Maine!
https://www.newscentermaine.com/article/news/local/207/207-interview/what-led-a-writer-to-the-amish/97-5d22729f-9cd0-4358-809d-305e7324f8f1

Novels by Ashley Emma on Amazon
USA Today Bestselling Author

GET 4 OF ASHLEY EMMA'S AMISH EBOOKS FOR FREE

www.AshleyEmmaAuthor.com

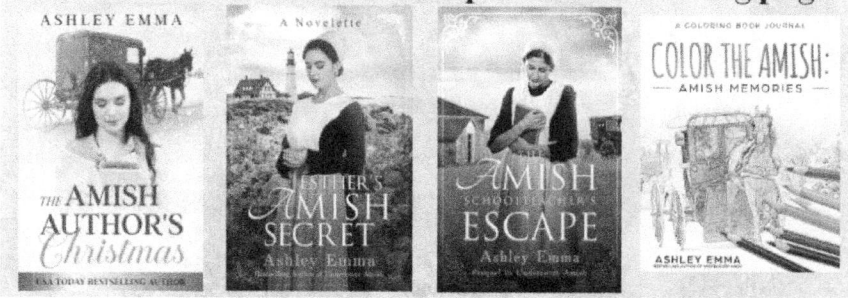

Your free ebook novellas and printable coloring pages

All of Ashley Emma's Books on Amazon

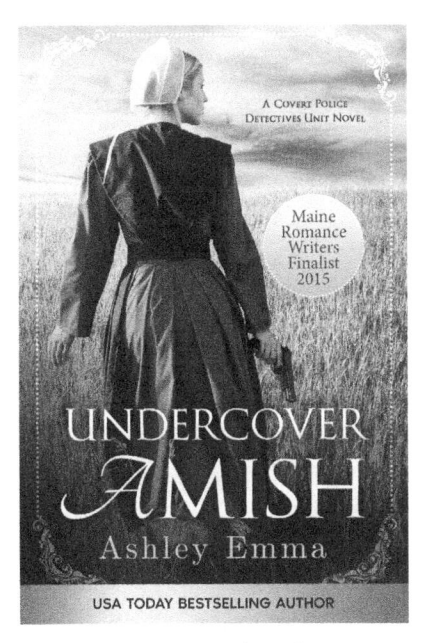

(This series can be read out of order or as standalone novels.)

Detective Olivia Mast would rather run through gunfire than return to her former Amish community in Unity, Maine, where she killed her abusive husband in self-defense.

Olivia covertly investigates a murder there while protecting the man she dated as a teen: Isaac Troyer, a potential target.

When Olivia tells Isaac she is a detective, will he be willing to break Amish rules to help her arrest the killer?

Undercover Amish was a finalist in Maine Romance Writers Strut Your Stuff Competition 2015 where it received 26 out of 27 points and has 455+ Amazon reviews!

Buy here: https://www.amazon.com/Ashley-Emma/e/B00IYTZTQE/

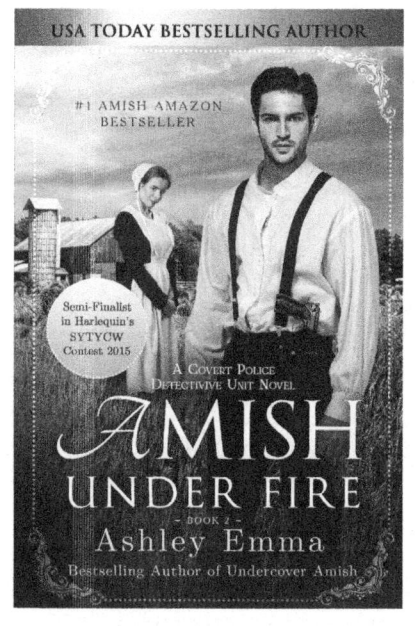

After Maria Mast's abusive ex-boyfriend is arrested for being involved in sex trafficking and modern-day slavery, she thinks that she and her son Carter can safely return to her Amish community.

But the danger has only just begun.

Someone begins stalking her, and they want blood and revenge.

Agent Derek Turner of Covert Police Detectives Unit is assigned as her bodyguard and goes with her to her Amish community in Unity, Maine.

Maria's secretive eyes, painful past, and cautious demeanor intrigue him.

As the human trafficking ring begins to target the Amish community, Derek wonders if the distraction of her will cost him his career...and Maria's life.

Buy on Amazon: https://www.amazon.com/Ashley-Emma/e/B00IYTZTQE/

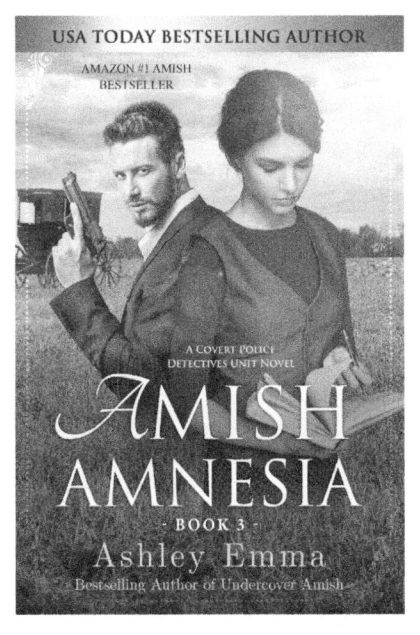

When Officer Jefferson Martin witnesses a young woman being hit by a car near his campsite, all thoughts of vacation vanish as the car speeds off.

When the malnourished, battered woman wakes up, she can't remember anything before the accident. They don't know her name, so they call her Jane.

When someone breaks into her hospital room and tries to kill her before getting away, Jefferson volunteers to protect Jane around the clock. He takes her back to their Kennebunkport beach house along with his upbeat sister Estella and his friend who served with him overseas in the Marine Corps, Ben Banks.

At first, Jane's stalker leaves strange notes, but then his attacks become bolder and more dangerous.

Buy on Amazon:
https://www.amazon.com/Ashley-Emma/e/B00IYTZTQE/

Threatened. Orphaned. On the run.

With no one else to turn to, these two terrified sisters can only hope their Amish aunt will take them in. But the quaint Amish community of Unity, Maine, is not as safe as it seems.

After Charlotte Cooper's parents die and her abusive ex-fiancé threatens her, the only way to protect her younger sister Zoe is by faking their deaths and leaving town.

The sisters' only hope of a safe haven lies with their estranged Amish aunt in Unity, Maine, where their mother grew up before she left the Amish.

Elijah Hochstettler, the family's handsome farmhand, grows closer to Charlotte as she digs up dark family secrets that her mother kept from her.

Buy on Amazon here: https://www.amazon.com/Ashley-Emma/e/B00IYTZTQE/

When nurse Anna Hershberger finds a man with a bullet wound who begs her to help him without taking him to the hospital, she has a choice to make.

Going against his wishes, she takes him to the hospital to help him after he passes out. She thinks she made the right decision...until an assassin storms in with a gun. Anna has no choice but to go on the run with her patient.

This handsome stranger, who says his name is Connor, insists that they can't contact the police for help because there are moles leaking information. His mission is to shut down a local sex trafficking ring targeting Anna's former Amish community in Unity, Maine, and he needs her help most of all.

Since Anna was kidnapped by sex traffickers in her Amish community, she would love nothing more than to get justice and help put the criminals behind bars.

But can she trust Connor to not get her killed? And is he really who he says he is?

Buy on Amazon:
https://www.amazon.com/Ashley-Emma/e/B00IYTZTQE/

Ever wondered what it would be like to live in an Amish community? Now you can find out in this true story with photos.

Buy on Amazon: https://www.amazon.com/Ashley-Emma/e/B00IYTZTQE/

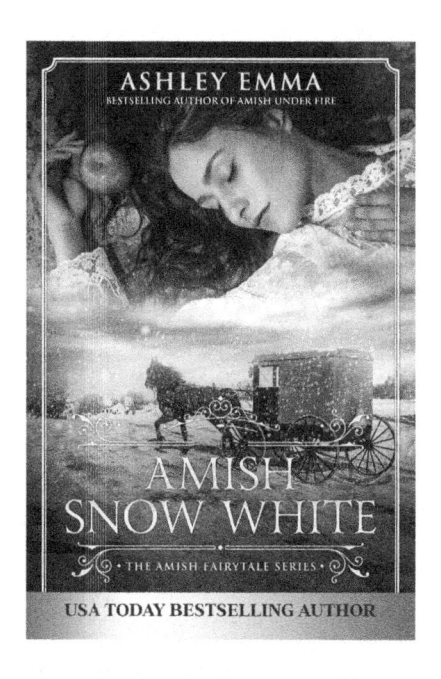

An heiress on the run.

A heartbroken Amish man, sleep-walking through life.

Can true love's kiss break the spell?

After his wife dies and he returns to his Amish community, Dominic feels numb and frozen, like he's under a spell.

When he rescues a woman from a car wreck in a snowstorm, he brings her home to his mother and six younger siblings. They care for her while she sleeps for several days, and when she wakes up in a panic, she pretends to have amnesia.

But waking up is only the beginning of Snow's story.

Buy on Amazon:

https://www.amazon.com/Ashley-Emma/e/B00IYTZTQE/

She's an Amish beauty with a love of reading, hiding a painful secret. He's a reclusive, scarred military hero who won't let anyone in. Can true love really be enough?

On her way home from the bookstore, Belle's buggy crashes in front of the old mansion that everyone else avoids, of all places.

What she finds inside the mansion is not a monster, but a man. Scarred both physiologically and physically by the horrors of military combat, Cole's burned and disfigured face tells the story of all he lost to the war in a devastating explosion.

He's been hiding from the world ever since.

After Cole ends up hiring her as his housekeeper and caretaker for his firecracker of a grandmother, Belle can't help her curiosity as she wonders what exactly Cole does in his office all day.

Why is Cole's office so off-limits to Belle? What is he hiding in there?

https://www.amazon.com/Ashley-Emma/e/B00IYTZTQE/

Abraham and Sarah know in their hearts that they are meant to have children, but what if they are wrong? And if they are meant to have children, how will God make it possible?

Just when all seems lost, God once again answers their prayers in a miraculous and unexpected way that begins a new chapter in their lives.

In this emotional family saga, experience hope and inspiration through this beloved Bible story retold.

https://www.amazon.com/Abraham-Sarahs-Amish-Baby-family-ebook/dp/B09DWCBD7M

Gomer is not your typical Amish woman.
On the outside, Gomer seems like a lovely, sweet, young Amish woman, but she's hiding a scandalous secret.

Gomer was created to sing. Most of all, she loves to sing on stage for the audience--she loves the applause, the lights, and the performance--**but her Amish community forbids it.**

How can Hosea find his wife, bring her home, and piece their family back together again when it seems impossible?

https://www.amazon.com/Hosea-Gomers-Amish-Secret-family-ebook/dp/B09GQVCBM9

When Ruth's husband Mahlon dies one morning on his way out the door, she thinks she will never find love again--but little does she know that God has a miraculous plan for her future.

In Unity, Ruth catches the eye of successful farmer Boaz Petersheim. He's drawn to her not only because of her beauty, but because of her loyalty and devotion to her mother-in-law, Naomi. When Ruth asks for a job harvesting wheat in his fields, he immediately hires her because he can see how much she wants to take care of her mother-in-law, even though she is the only female worker among his male employees.

When rumors sweep through the community after a near-death experience, who will Boaz believe?
https://www.amazon.com/gp/product/B09M7XV76C

Excerpt of Abraham and Sarah's Amish Baby

Chapter One

Abraham Lehman hummed a hymn as he rode his buggy down the dirt lane, stopping in front of his small, humble home—a sturdy little maroon house that he would have filled with children years ago if he had ever gotten married. He'd always dreamed of falling in love with the right woman and raising a large family.

Maybe it's time to accept that it's not your plan for me, Lord, he whispered, sorrow weighing down his heart. *I'm not getting any younger. What woman would want to marry me at my age?*

He jumped down from his horse, slapping his boots hard on the ground. He removed the straw hat that shaded the top half of his face from the brutal heat of the sun. His tall, broad-shouldered shadow loomed on the dirt driveway as he ran his work-worn hands through his salt and pepper hair.

At forty-three years old, he was still lean and strong. Working on his father's farm had callused and toughened his hands. His horse neighed and Abraham laughed, stroking his black, thick mane.

A gray-haired woman named Eva and her daughter, Catherine, were walking down the lane, talking animatedly. They stopped when they saw Abraham, smiling sheepishly at him.

"Good morning, Eva and Catherine," he said in a cheerful voice, waving.

"Good morning, Abraham." Catherine greeted him enthusiastically, her eyes looking him over hungrily from head to toe, then lingering a little longer than necessary on his face. She was in her mid-thirties, and though she could catch the eye of the younger single men in town, she seemed to be set on getting Abraham to notice her.

Abraham walked around to the other side of his horse, trying not to cringe under her gaze.

"Oh, Abraham, you must come home with us. We have the raspberries I promised you. I picked them yesterday, just for you," Catherine said. "I know how much you love them."

Abraham blinked. Did she just bat her eyelashes at me?

"That is so kind of you, Catherine, but really, you don't have to do that for me." He didn't want her to think that he meant anything by accepting them—and he sure didn't want to feel indebted to her.

"It's nothing, Abraham. Come on. It's not like our house is far away," she said, striding off toward the house she shared with her parents, not giving him the chance to turn her down. Eva waddled behind her.

He fought the urge to roll his eyes and groan. Reluctantly, he followed the two women down the lane to their house, leading his horse.

"Hello there, Abraham!" Aaron Smith, Eva's husband, called. He waved from where he sat on the porch, reading a book.

"Hello, Aaron. Lovely day, isn't it?" Abraham asked.

"Come on inside!" Eva called over her shoulder as she hurried up the steps to the two-story tan house. Vibrant flower bushes bloomed in front of the house under the windows.

Abraham tied his horse's bridle to the post, then walked inside. The kitchen had the overwhelming smell of baked pastries and cookies. Abraham wondered if Catherine had made her famous cookies. He didn't admire many of Catherine's traits, but he had to admit she was an excellent cook and baker.

He inhaled deeply. In moments like these, he was actively aware of his bachelorhood. If he were married, he'd enjoy his home smelling like this. A deep sigh rumbled from somewhere deep within him.

Catherine was leaning on the door frame, watching him. She quirked one eyebrow. He jumped slightly when she spoke.

"I made those cookies you love. I'll wrap some of them for you," she said, smiling coyly.

"You don't have to, Catherine," he said dismissively.

"Oh please," she said, waving him off. "It's the least we can do after the repairs you've done for us around the house. My father appreciates it too, even though he wishes he could make the repairs himself like he used to." She placed the crate of eggs from the Smiths' chickens on the table next to the basket of berries, then proceeded to wrap up some cookies.

"Thank you," he said quietly, not bothering to argue with her. Besides, he did love those cookies.

Abraham left the kitchen, not wanting to spend another second alone with Catherine. Her tireless flirting exhausted him. Even though he had explained to her that he wasn't interested in her, she refused to leave him alone. He liked the Smith family, but he didn't care about Catherine in a romantic way at all.

Eva now stood in the garden, smelling her flowers.

"Thank you for the raspberries, Mrs. Smith," Abraham said, a polite smile on his face.

"For the umpteenth time, you can call me Eva," she said, wagging her finger.

Abraham chuckled.

"I'm serious. 'Mrs. Smith' makes me feel old. I am not old. I'm only sixty-eight." Eva stood tall, arms crossed, hiking her chin.

"Yes, Eva. I'll try to remember that."

"Good then." She nodded, then inspected her flowers.

Aaron guffawed. "Oh, we are getting old, alright. That's why it takes me so long to get up out of my chair these days."

Abraham chuckled, then turned when something caught his eye. There were signs of life in the once empty house across the lane. The garden was no longer brown and brittle—now it was green with life. The outer part of the building was painted gray.

"Did someone move into Old Mr. Paul's house?" he asked Eva.

The kitchen window was open. A beautiful woman in a black Amish dress and white apron swept the floor. Her long, uncovered, marvelous red hair swayed around her hips as she moved. Clearly, she was alone, because she wore no prayer kapp. At some point, she stopped to tuck some of it behind her ears, revealing her pretty face—pensive eyes, a delicately curved nose, and full, pink lips.

Abraham's heart leapt, and he fought the urge to run over there and introduce himself immediately. What was her name? He needed to know.

Eva's voice jolted his thoughts. "I believe so. I've gone over, but she pretended to not be home. I don't think the woman is keen on making friends."

"I had no idea Old Paul's house had been sold," Abraham murmured.

"She insists on keeping to herself. I haven't even seen her go to town for supplies or groceries, and she's been here for over a week," Catherine chipped in. Abraham had no idea when she came out from the kitchen.

"Some people like peace and quiet instead of constant chatter," Aaron chimed in from the porch, but his wife and daughter ignored him.

"I did see her outside doing yard work and she was wearing a prayer *kapp*, so she's Amish, but she hasn't been to church yet. She doesn't seem enthusiastic about getting to know her neighbors," Eva observed, peering at the house, clearly oblivious to Aaron's comment.

"She doesn't seem to want to meet anyone," Catherine agreed with a wave of her hand.

"Why do you think that is?" Abraham asked, extremely curious. He couldn't take his eyes off her.

"Perhaps she is like that plain old Mrs. Matthews. Remember how she died up at her cottage in the woods alone and no one knew until Dave's golden retriever found her?" Eva reflected.

"I remember. That was so terrible." Abraham shook his head.

"Well, I think she's a loner like Mrs. Matthews," Catherine said. "I just hope nothing happens to her."

"You two worry too much. She's probably just shy!" Aaron called from the porch. "Don't go scaring her away, constantly trying to bring over your cookies."

"Everyone loves my cookies. Don't they, Abraham?" Catherine eyed him, waiting for his reply.

"Of course." Abraham smiled at Aaron, who rolled his eyes, then turned back to his book.

He studied the strange new woman. Silently, he willed her to look out of the window. As if in an answer, she gazed out of the window and looked straight at Abraham. They locked eyes. She wiped her eye with her hand. Was she crying? Something stirred inside Abraham. Though she was across the lane, he could see that her eyes held a quiet intrigue. Could she see all the questions in his eyes?

"Speaking of cookies, here are your berries, eggs, and cookies, Abraham," Catherine said, once again jolting him from his thoughts.

Abraham turned to her, taking them. "Thanks." When Catherine's hand lingered on his for too long, he stumbled backward to get away from her touch.

"Be careful with those raspberries. They took me a while to pick, so you better not drop them," Catherine said in a playful tone, seemingly oblivious.

"I will be."

"I'm always careful, Abraham. That's one of the things I like about myself. Maybe if you got to know me better, you'd know that too," Catherine said flirtatiously in a low voice.

Either Eva hadn't heard her, or was pretending not to hear as she weeded her garden. "You know, you should go introduce yourself to our new neighbor."

"If she answers the door," Aaron added.

"Yes. I believe I will try," Abraham said, moving toward his horse, glad for the excuse to leave.

"Oh, what a lovely idea," Catherine said. "We'll go with you." She started walking across the lane, her mother on her heels.

Aaron guffawed again from the porch. "Now she definitely won't open the door."

Maybe Aaron was right. Abraham fought the urge to groan again. How would he ever get away from these two meddling neighbors?

***

The stairs creaked loudly as forty-year-old Sarah Fisher descended the steps of her new home. Well, it was new to her, but in reality, it seemed like it was two hundred years old.

In her right hand swung a bucket that she found in the attic upstairs, and in the other hand, she held a mop.

She looked up at the ceiling, biting her lip. Drips fell from the ceiling onto the floor, forming a puddle that seeped underneath her woodstove. Speaking of cooking, she made a mental note to go shopping for groceries and other supplies sometime soon. She didn't have to open her fridge to know that all it contained was some old cheese and a casserole that a neighbor had so kindly left on the front porch when Sarah hadn't had the courage to answer the door. One day, she'd find that neighbor and thank her, but not today.

As she crossed the living room into the kitchen, she noticed the soullessness of the house. The living room was still unfurnished and bereft of any signs that indicated someone lived there. Most of the boxes containing her belongings had not been unpacked yet, even though it had been almost a week since she moved to Smyrna.

The silence of her house disoriented her. There were no kids running around, tugging on her skirt, even though she wished there were. She was always aware of how largely unfulfilled her life was. She was still unmarried, with no potential suitors in sight. She deeply yearned to settle down and build a large family of her own. She wanted to cook for them, take care of her husband, and read to children of her own. At forty, she wasn't getting any younger. The loneliness of being an only child contributed immensely to her desire to have many kids. Growing up, she yearned for siblings to play and fight with.

Looking out of the window, she was once again reminded of why she chose this town. Birds sang beautiful tunes from the surrounding treetops. The sound of bleating goats blended with that of mooing cows. The air was crisp and clean. She took a deep breath in, filling her lungs with the smell of new beginnings.

The first night Sarah moved to the town, a woman had stopped by with a gift basket and a charming smile. At first, Sarah had pretended she wasn't home, running and hiding when the woman had knocked on the door.

"I know you're in there, dear. Don't be shy. I'm Eva, your new neighbor. I just want to welcome you to the community. I live across the road," she'd said in a beautiful, lilting voice. "I have a gift for you. Won't you open the door?"

How could Sarah resist? She crept to the door, smoothed a hand over her uncovered hair, and opened it a crack.

"Oh, I don't mind if your hair is uncovered. Trust me. I used to be a midwife. I've delivered many babies, both human and animal. I've lived enough life to not be fazed by the sight of an Amish woman's uncovered head." Eva laughed out loud at her own joke, and Sarah couldn't help but smile. Maybe she would like this woman.

A few days had gone by since that night, and now Sarah watched her neighbors talking in their yard. They seemed more like friends than mother and daughter. Seeing them made her heart sink. Theirs was the kind of friendship she never had with her deceased mother.

Her heart plummeted at the thoughts of her parents invading her mind. Images of the friendship she and her father shared came back to her. She shook her head to dislodge the memories.

She stepped away from the window to focus on mopping the hardwood floor when her thoughts started straying to the cause of her father's death. She concentrated on soaking up the water, her hands working together in harmony. Her arms, stretched and taut, worked furiously. She gathered the soaking ends of her black dress and apron.

Her father's favorite Bible verse wandered into her mind as she cleaned: When you pass through the waters, I will be with you.

She recited the verse quietly in her mind as she worked. She remembered those times when her father repeated it to her during her low moments. Even as a child suffering terrifying nightmares, her father would read that verse to calm her.

"Remember, Sarah, you're God's child. He will always be with you. The next time you have those nightmares, remember this verse," he'd say.

A tear dropped from Sarah's eyes, her heart filling with sorrow. She sniffed and shook her head, trying to push the memories out of her mind.

She looked out of the window and locked eyes with a man who was talking with Eva and her daughter. She instantly felt drawn to him. Even though he was across the lane, she felt like his eyes were gazing right into hers.

Who is that?

They started walking toward her house.

Oh, no. They were coming over here to see her. Her heart raced in a panic, her hands flying to pull her unfettered, knee-length hair into a bun.

She'd seem rude if she didn't answer the door now. They'd clearly seen her. Now they were headed to her front door.

She hurried out of the kitchen. The kitchen floor almost glowed, but her uncovered red hair was another matter. This time, it wouldn't just be Eva at her door. That man would be joining them, and she would have to have her hair covered before they arrived.

As Sarah scrambled to put her hair in a haphazard bun, quickly pinning it in place before pulling on her *kapp*, the knock came sooner than she expected. Hoping she looked half-decent, she smoothed a hand over the hairs peeking out from her head covering. She also quickly scrubbed her hands over her face, hoping there were no longer any smudges of dirt on her. She took a deep breath before opening the door.

Their smiling faces confronted Sarah: the blue-eyed man, gray-haired woman, and her daughter, who was smiling at her in a strange way, almost as if she was faking it. So, these were her new neighbors.

Sarah's eyes met the man's gaze, and now that he was closer... Oh, my, was he ever handsome. His sky-blue eyes were framed by his salt-and-pepper hair, a slightly pointed nose, and a friendly smile. Only the color of his hair gave away his age, along with a few lines near his eyes, but they were more endearing than anything, marking a long life full of joy. His shirt sleeves were rolled up to his elbows in the summer sun, and a quick glimpse of his muscular forearms had her heart racing, filling her stomach with fluttering butterflies—something she hadn't felt in years.

What is wrong with me? I'm a grown woman, not some lovestruck teenager, she thought. *I don't even know this man.*

"Hello, Sarah. How are you? This is my daughter, Catherine, and this is our friend, Abraham." Eva flashed another charming smile. "He lives just down the lane."

"Hello. How lovely to meet you, Catherine and Abraham," Sarah said, nodding. "Please come in." She opened the door wide. She ushered them into her bare-walled living room. They sank into the cane chairs, the only furniture available.

"I'm sorry the place looks uninhabited. I just moved in."

"Oh, that's okay, dear," Eva said. "I know how much work moving into a new community can be. About thirty years ago, Aaron and I moved here from our hometown in Tennessee," Eva chirped. "It took a long time to feel at home, but now we certainly do."

Sarah nodded. "May I offer you something? Tea? Coffee? You have to forgive me if it takes time. I haven't—"

"Unpacked?" Catherine cut in.

Sarah cocked her head to study Catherine. She noticed the smug, self-satisfied smile on her almost perfect face, and how close she sat to the man, as though they were courting.

Are they courting? she wondered.

"Right. I am sorry, but—" Sarah started saying.

"It's okay, Sarah. You don't have to apologize," the man said.

His silky voice surprised Sarah. She imagined a tall, well-built man like that to have a deep, gravelly voice and not one that washed over a person so smoothly.

"Welcome to Smyrna. If you ever need anything, I'd be more than happy to help," he offered, and his smile made her look away. She self-consciously tucked a stray hair behind her ear.

What is wrong with me? she chided herself. "Thank you so much. So, tea, anyone?"

"I'll help you in the kitchen," Eva offered, standing up.

"You don't have to."

"I insist. I want to get to know you, and what better way to bond than over a kitchen counter?" Eva asked, following her.

Sarah smiled. The older lady had a way of talking her way through everything. In the corner of her eye, Sarah noticed Catherine reaching for Abraham's hand as they left the room.

Her heart sank to her toes. So, it's true. They must be courting, after all.

Why was she so disappointed? She didn't even know this man, and it was none of her business.

In the kitchen, Eva started up the woodstove. She put the kettle on, as chatty as ever. Sarah struggled to keep up with the conversation as she brought out the cups and spoons from boxes in the corner.

"You must let me make you my famous cookies. If you have them with tea, it's heavenly, I tell you."

Sarah's eyes filled as she remembered her own mother's delicious cookies. Pictures of her mother dressed in a white apron over her gown, white flour sprinkled across the sides of her face, kneading the flour, mixing butter, and breaking eggs into bowls in the kitchen filled Sarah's mind. The sweet smell of baked cookies that filled the house, how those cookies tasted, and the sound of them crunching between her teeth cascaded through her senses.

She recalled the look of delight on her father's face whenever he ate them. Oh, how she missed her mother and father.

"Really? I must try them then," Sarah said, managing a weak smile.

"Peter down at the store has tried to get me to bake some cookies to sell, but I am getting too old for that kind of job. The women in church never tire of trying to get me to reveal my recipe, but it's a secret passed down in my family for generations." Eva's voice beamed with pride.

Sarah smiled at the woman's excitement. She understood where her pride came from. Sarah's own mother had been proud of her excellent home-keeping and cooking skills. Motherhood was the only thing Sarah wanted out of life: to be able to feel the fulfillment of raising children, but she'd never found the right man to marry.

Her mind involuntarily turned to the short-haired, blue-eyed man with the beardless face in her living room. He seemed slightly older than she was, with an intriguing face. But that wasn't what had caught Sarah's attention. There was something about him, the way he made her feel. She tried to bury it—she didn't think she was ready for another courtship. She needed to concentrate on dealing with the guilt and grief of her parents' death, healing and moving on from that.

Yet, the thought of him and Catherine together troubled her for some reason. He didn't seem as keen as Catherine. He didn't pay her nearly as much attention as she did to him. She wondered if he was the kind who married mainly out of fulfilling the obligations expected of him and not of love.

But if that was true, wouldn't he have married years ago? Perhaps, like her, he would not marry until he knew it was right. Maybe he was still waiting for just the right person to come along.

"Are you listening to me, dear?" Eva asked loudly.

Sarah blinked back to the present. "Yes, of course, Eva."

Eva studied her for a minute with a penetrating gaze that made Sarah uncomfortable. "I asked about your husband. Will he be joining you soon?"

Sarah swallowed hard. "No."

"And why's that?"

"I am not married," she said, a tinge of sadness in her voice.

"Oh, well then. Can I let you in on a secret?" Eva asked in a lowered voice, a mischievous grin on her face. "There are lots of eligible bachelors here. Some may be widowers with children, but still, you won't have any trouble finding a husband here, Sarah."

"So... Are Catherine and Abraham courting?" Sarah asked hesitantly.

"Well, not officially, but I believe Abraham and Catherine might be getting together soon. Abraham is such a wonderful man. I'd be lucky to have him as a son-in-law," Eva beamed.

Sarah nodded, her heart sinking even farther down, through the worn floorboards.

"What's wrong, dear? You've barely left this house since you moved in. You try to hide it, but I can see the sadness written all over you. So, tell me, what happened to you? Why did you move here? What are you running away from?"

Sarah had vowed to keep her grief to herself, but the sincerity in the old woman's eyes compelled her to start speaking. "I lost my parents recently. I'm still grieving."

She paused and clenched her fist. She could feel the tears coming. She wouldn't cry here; not now, not ever. The scripture came back to her: When you pass through the waters, I will be with you.

Peace flooded her heart. Grief would not sweep over her.

A tear fell from her eye. She wiped it with the back of her hand and shook her head furiously.

Eva handed her a napkin to clean her eyes with and patted her on the back. "Child, the good Lord does not give us more than we can handle. Remember that and know that you'll get through this."

Sarah covered her face with the napkin and let the tears out. A few minutes later, she managed to sober up. She sniffled and wiped her running nose.

"Sarah, I want to thank you for trusting me with this. I know it must be hard to talk about."

"Please don't tell anyone," Sarah said, clasping her hands together. "I don't want anyone feeling bad for me."

"Of course." Eva made a gesture of zipping her lips.

The kettle started whistling, steam snaking out through every opening.

***

Abraham's thoughts stayed with Sarah long after she left the living room. He thought about the symmetry of her face, her high cheekbones, curved nose, full lips, and her fair skin. He tried to concentrate on her voice and the depth of her eyes. He wanted to know the secret that was eating away at her soul. He wanted to know the reason for the great sadness that she was doing such a poor job hiding.

But Catherine's voice kept cutting through his imagination. Abraham wished she would go to the other room or keep quiet for a minute.

"Come on, Abraham. What could go wrong?" she asked.

I can think of a million things that can go wrong. "Look, Catherine…"

"Before you say it, Abraham, just listen to my proposition," Catherine cut in.

He sighed. "Okay, let's hear it."

"Let's go on three trial dates. Just three dates. If at the end of the third date, you still don't want to court me, I'll respect your wish."

Abraham furrowed his brows, doubtful that she would ever accept no for an answer.

"Come on, Abraham," Catherine pleaded in a coy voice.

"Fine. I guess I can do that." Maybe if he finally went on three dates with her, she would see just how much they were not right for each other, how there was no spark.

Catherine squealed happily, clapping her hands together. "How about Tuesday evening? At David's Café?"

Abraham nodded, suddenly feeling like he'd made a huge mistake, but there was no backing out now.

"Trust me, Abraham. You won't ever regret this," she promised.

Sure. Abraham kept quiet. She continued talking animatedly, but he had tuned her out. To get his attention, Catherine grabbed his hand, but Abraham jerked away as if her touch had scalded him.

Just then, Sarah and Eva appeared, bearing trays filled with cups of tea.

"What are you two talking about?" Eva asked, raising an eyebrow.

"Abraham and I are going on a date on Tuesday," Catherine announced, her voice a little too high.

"How lovely is that?" Eva beamed. "Finally! This is wonderful."

A look of confusion and sadness crossed Sarah's face, but was quickly replaced with what seemed like a forced smile. "That's great news."

Her face said otherwise. Was it just him, or was Sarah just as unhappy about the date as he was?

****

If you enjoyed this sample, check out Abraham and Sarah's Amish Baby on Amazon here in ebook and paperback:
https://www.amazon.com/gp/product/B09DWCBD7M/ref=dbs_a_def_rwt_bibl_vppi_i1

Made in the USA
Monee, IL
24 August 2023